CU00869032

'I am Soldier'
II Para

Copyright © David Hull

Edited by Emma Hardcastle

Cover design by Christian Turford

Cover photo: Pro Operational 2nd Rupert Frere,
Sgt Rupert Frere RLC, Crown Copyright.
Paratrooper from 2nd Para keeps watch from the
roof of a compound in Afghanistan.

Every young man has a choice; you could buy a beret for £20 or you can sweat 20lbs and earn it the hard way and feel proud to join the brotherhood.

This is to all the men who have tried
and failed Para training.

It's better to have tried and failed,
then not to have tried at all.

Chapter 1

He ran forward with purpose, his beating heart resonating in his ears. He could hear his short heavy breaths as he fought desperately to drag the warm night air in and out of his lungs faster than God had intended; all to the sound of crunching boots in the dirt at either side of his position.

After a short jog he came to the first hut, made from sticks, straw and mud. It had probably stood the test of time twice over. The people of Africa had resided here for many years and had only ever known poverty and war. To them, hearing gun fire was as common as a siren from any of the emergency services; those everyday background noises a Brit wouldn't respond to.

His thighs, thick and muscular, and his calves, burning with the build up of lactic acid, throbbed as his blood pumped faster. He kicked the door of the closest hut practically off its hinges with one massive effort, before pointing his rifle in through the entrance and letting off half a dozen rounds. Seconds later, when no fire was returned, he swung into the doorway taking up its width with his broad shoulders.

Seeing movement in one of the dark corners, he let rip with another burst of between ten and twenty rounds. When the scream of the resident alarmed him, he carried out a quick search

4

before exiting and charging onto the next hut.

The clearing of the village, consisting of forty huts, took around thirty minutes for the Company of men. Those in question were all members of the British Army's second battalion Parachute Regiment (2 Para). Twenty six enemy dead, three women and sixty six hostages, most of whom were of no importance to the Army Commanders who'd planned and led the raid.

The raid was a message to the militia operating in this area, they ran the region with an iron fist and to rule was to put fear in all by killing remorselessly. They did not discriminate, men, women, even children would be killed for the pettiest of crimes. Intelligence had come in from a small unit of soldiers belonging to the British Special Air Service (SAS) that at least three of the leaders lived in this village along with supporters of their cause. The British Military decided to send them a message. Genocide will not be tolerated and fire would be met with fire.

The Paras suffered one injury and no fatalities. The injured Paratrooper was slightly embarrassed by his plight and in true military fashion his comrades wasted no time in mocking his state. Mike Spence was twenty one years old and had been a member of 2 Para for the last twelve months. This was his first active service and he wanted to make a good impression. He needed to prove he was the fastest, most aggressive trooper in the company.

As he approached his first hut he stumbled on a large rock and tumbled forwards, knocking himself unconscious for a few minutes before clambering back to his feet and carrying on with the operation. He found no enemy in the three huts he eventually cleared as its residents had already fled. But as the soldiers stood-to after the operation and the Chinook had been called in for the evacuation, they noticed Mike with his battered and bruised face and joked about how it was 'nice of him to drop by'. Mike took the abuse on the chin and responded with his fingers.

Standing amongst the men was Corporal Kenny King, the first man to hit the huts. Kenny was five feet ten inches tall and weighed exactly fourteen stone; his face was round with deep brown eyes and full lips; he had joined the Paras at the age of seventeen and a half which made him a young soldier. His reputation amongst the men of 2 Para was a formidable one. In his six years with the regiment he had seen active service four times, and these included Northern Ireland (NI), Iraq, Afghanistan, South Africa and now here in North Africa. In his youth he had been quite chubby and although no-one ever physically bullied him, he was tired of struggling with his weight. It had served him well on the school rugby team and got him noticed early on in basic training at Aldershot.

Kenny, like many men joining the

Parachute Regiment, had lofty aspirations of one day becoming a member of the elite SAS. Most never attempt the selection due to its formidable reputation for breaking the hardest of men regardless of what regiment they came from. For those who did, only a small portion would make the rank of Trooper in what is considered the toughest fighting force in the world. Most figured it was better not to try at all than to try and fail because the embarrassment of being returned to unit (RTU'd) was too great. He was happy for the time being to be part of the Paras and hoped to become a Sergeant in the next two or three years.

Unlike most Paras, Kenny didn't say much. His quiet demeanour added to his already tough persona. Private Richard Black was his closest friend; they were nicknamed the Siamese twins as they were rarely seen apart.

Richard was a tough Scotsman from Grangemouth, Falkirk; he was of slim build with a gaunt face and piercing blue eyes. His father was an ex Para who spent eighteen years with 3 Para before being medically discharged after a parachuting accident, breaking his back in three places. His untimely retirement from the Army played hard on the family. It broke his heart which hurt more than the injury itself. He was a heavy drinker and began beating his wife and two sons.

Richard was the youngest by four years and his brother Simon ran away from home at sixteen and was found dead some weeks later in London after a glue sniffing incident Richard rarely spoke of. It devastated the family further, and as soon as Richard was sixteen years old his mother agreed to sign the consent forms and he joined the junior Army.

Kenny stood with dirt swirling around his desert combat boots with his colleagues as the sun began to rise. He knew the soaring temperatures wouldn't be far behind. Some of the soldiers smoked as they chatted, others taunted the prisoners by calling them names or prodding them with the barrel of their rifles. Members of two section continued to pour scorn on poor Mike Spence while three section- Kenny's section- watched the Northern perimeter.

As the Chinook came into sight and the prisoners were dragged to their feet, one spoke directly to Kenny.

"What are you?" the man said in broken English.

Kenny looked at him, pausing for a moment. He responded in a similar broken English style.

"I am this," he said with a slight smile on his face, while pointing to a small tattoo of a Chinese symbol on his left forearm.

"What is this meaning?" he asked, puzzled.

"I am Soldier," he responded.

The tough expression on Kenny's face said it all. He meant business.

"You good soldier?" asked the man.

Kenny nodded to the man before they were interrupted by his friend Black.

"Yeah man, we're the fucking best in the world. We're the red devils!"

The man looked angry by this comment and spat in Black's face, who in return lurched forward to attack. Kenny grabbed his arm, preventing him from moving more than a couple of inches.

"Let it go Rich," he said calmly.

"Fucking piece of shit! Who does he think he is?" growled Black.

"He's a guy who not more than an hour ago was enjoying his kip, when a bunch of fucking madmen came bursting through his lounge."

Black and the others around them burst out laughing.

"I never thought of it like that," said Black laughing along.

Kenny had calmed the situation without much of an effort. Once everyone was safely on the Chinook the remaining villagers were set free and returned to their damaged homes. The men of 2 Para clambered into the Chinook thinking only of a cool shower and their beds; maybe the chance of some food, or to the Army, hot scoff.

The Chinook landed at base camp and everyone exited the machine calmly as if getting off the number four bus. It didn't look like the mean machine carrying some of the toughest soldiers in the world. They ambled over to their hanger on the West side of the camp. This was designated the "Maroon" zone and only to be entered by the Para's themselves. They'd put up a sign saying, "Crap Hats Do Not Enter!!" A crap hat, or so they said, was anyone other than the Para's, even those who had completed the all arms Para training were still considered outsiders, and made unwelcome.

Kenny & Rich walked into the hanger together and sat on their beds. The heat was reaching thirty degrees centigrade. Sweat was running through his short brown hair and down Kenny's face. He sat staring at his feet for a while just watching the sand and dust slowly cascade off his boots. He seemed mesmerised by it. Rich noticed his friend doing this and quickly cut in, breaking the silence.

"Hey Kenny my old boy," he said putting on a posh accent. "Are you waiting for gunger din the servant boy to come and remove your footwear?"

Kenny smiled and looked up at him, "Yes actually I fucking well am.........now as my bitch I suggest you take them off for me and brush the sand off in said direction," he gestured ahead of him.

The tannoy system on site left a lot to be desired. A 1970's radio speaker set on a metal pole in the middle of camp. The camp housed over 400 men and women of the British Army and RAF. The speaker crackled into life stopping most people in their tracks as they had to listen carefully to understand what was being said.

"Standby, Standby.....This is not a drill!" the man's voice said in a firm tone. "All Para platoons report to the Heli landing pad immediately. Webbing, weapons and ammo. That's all."

The men jumped to their feet and grabbed their kit; Kenny was already out of the tent by the time the announcement had finished looking for his Commanding Officer (CO). He ran towards the landing pad at full speed constantly looking around as he went to observe the actions of those around him. As he reached the landing pad he saw his CO, Captain Malcolm Silvers, and slowed to a jog as he approached.

"Boss," he said as he got within a few feet of him. "What's the score?"

"Hi King, you'll find out soon enough but here's a quick overview. That village we hit earlier had connections as we suspected, so the militia have gone on the attack and burned down a neighbouring village, killing civilians. We're going in to kick some ass and see what's left to rescue. It's gonna be a real shit fest Corporal (Cpl)." He turned away to speak to the Senior Non Commissioned Officers (SNCO's) about the battle plan. King would have to wait to be briefed by the Sergeants (Sgts) once they were in the air or loaded on the trucks.

Within twenty minutes the battalion was ready to

go and four Chinook's came in to land and collect the platoons. The noise from the helicopters was deafening and most ducked their heads even though they were nowhere near the propellers out of habit. When you approached a Heli you were always told to duck down low and run as fast as you could to the door before hurling yourself into its body, unless of course you were walking up the rear tailgate.

The majority of the platoons from second battalion were ushered into the Chinook's at speed but the Reconnaissance Platoon (Recce) was told to hang back for a further briefing. Kenny grabbed his section and took them to the briefing tent on the edge of the landing pad and shouted for two section to follow. Once there they stood awaiting their CO. The tent was dry and dusty; the smell of sweat lingered in the warm air.

"Okay gents, this is it. We're going in the trucks and are gonna hit several small villages along the way. The villages are either militia or their supporters. General Gooder is causing this fucking war and we need to put a boot up his arse. Questions?" He paused for two seconds before continuing, "Are you ready to go to war men?" he shouted aggressively.

"Yes boss," came the response from the sixteen strong unit stood before him.

The men of 1 section, Recce Platoon, were sent out on a local mission which the other sections hadn't been briefed on. All they knew was that the beast was awake; the beast being a whole Battalion of Paratroopers who were about to unleash hell on the militia in this North African province. Two section climbed into the back of the open top 7.5 tonne Bedford military trucks and made their weapons ready. Pte Sanders was sat near the back of the vehicles when he felt his hands and forearms aching; when he looked down at he was gripping his rifle so tight his fingers were white. Realising his nerves were getting the better of him he slowly released the tension and took a deep breath to calm himself down.

After 30 minutes they came to a small river and the trucks came to a halt. The Cpls and Sgts jumped out and went to the CO for orders, then returned to the trucks and told the men to get out and prepare for an assault. The sections split up and ran across the slow moving river which was knee deep for most and didn't cause any problems. They got to the other side and scurried up the embankment slowing as they neared the top.

Kenny took a sneak peak over the top and saw a small village. There he witnessed around thirty armed men and women preparing for battle. Time was of the essence and he didn't want to put his men at risk by waiting until the enemy were ready for an attack. He gave the hand signals to the other section to split in half and take the right and left flanks of the village. The left would cause a diversion by shooting a few scattered rounds high over the village, distracting the assailants while he took his section through the middle of the camp, hopefully wiping out the majority of the enemy. The other half of 2 section would cover them from the right.

The men lay against the embankment waiting for the order to go. Their hearts were beating fast, and hands were clammy as they prepared for what would surely be a vicious battle. King looked up to the right flank and gave them a slight nod, then did the same to the left. Shots resonated from the left flank causing the predicted diversion. King saw the enemy running towards the left flank, screaming at their comrades whilst grabbing their rifles. And there were as many women as men amongst the enemy! He knew that his men would find it hard to kill a woman, but he had faith in them and was sure they would do the job in hand.

He gave the signal and leapt up, charging over the top of the sandy bank and down into the village.
"Go! Go! Go!"

He fired his rifle as he ran, hitting three men in the back as they attempted to find the source of the original gun fire to the left. Black was close behind his friend and took down at least another six of the enemy before they got to the first cover, another clay and straw hut. There was noise inside and King called out, "Fix bayonets!"

He turned and kicked the door in, firing a short burst into the room. Nothing happened; he heard no cry of pain. Kenny swung into the door only to be confronted by a tall black woman, lunging towards him with a long wooden spear. His head swerved to the right in an attempt to avoid the weapon's strike, but it caught him across his left cheek, tearing through his flesh like a knife through butter.

In retaliation, he threw up a vicious front kick with his right leg, knocking her backwards across the floor of the hut. As she hit the ground he grabbed his rifle in both hands and lunged at her, jabbing his bayonet through her stomach and chest. Kenny exploded with fury, hitting her several times before realising what he had done. It all happened in the space of a few seconds, but he didn't have the time to mess about or stand there feeling remorse. Kill or be killed, that was all he needed to know.

He left her lying and moved towards more enemy personnel, firing from his shoulder three rounds to each person. His shooting was pin point accurate as one after another the militia fell.

Black crouched behind a large mound of mud next to a larger building made with more substantial materials. He fired his light support weapon (LSW) on rapid fire changing magazine after magazine as the battle raged on. He was sweating heavily in the heat; beads ran in his eyes, causing them to sting and blur his vision, but he carried on regardless.

He watched as the unit continued to charge forward, keeping the momentum of the attack going. He got up and ran forward to the next piece of cover, which turned out to be a wooden barrow- the kind a donkey would pull with the villager's supplies. Two members of the militia saw his move and turned their fire to him. Rounds bounced off the cart and the ground surrounding him. He was pinned.

The enemy fired their AK47 assault rifles at Black as he crouched behind the cart. He hoped someone would notice his plight soon, or he was going to have to get up and risk being shot in an attempt to move forward. The smell of manure filled his nostrils; it seemed to be coming from the cart. As he quickly popped his head around the corner to see if he could get a clear shot, he heard the whoosh of a under barrel grenade launcher (UGL) firing and two seconds later the enemy were no more.

Private Sandy McMann had noticed his colleague's position and took action, blowing the two men off their feet and critically injuring both. He didn't stop there. He ran forward firing from the hip putting half a dozen rounds into each of them.

Black got up and shouted playfully, "Cheers my old chap, jolly good of you to drop in."

In the midst of all the chaos they still

16

managed to keep their sense of humour.

Kenny and a young guy from 2 section worked together clearing the last few huts on the far side of the village. Private John Cassum was a thin young man but as tough as they came. He was born and bred in Newcastle and left home at 16 to join the Junior Army. He transferred into Para training at the age of seventeen and a half. He was twenty years old and had a lot of combat experience, so Kenny felt confident working with him.

The routine continued with Kenny kicking the hell out of the doors as Cassum threw in a grenade. Then they would both charge in, following the drills they had learned many years ago. The battle lasted ninety minutes in total. Once the dust had settled they gathered the bodies in one area and counted the dead. Forty three people had been killed by the Para's on this day, thirteen of which were women. When the troopers looked at those that had been killed, some tried to act tough by making comments such as, "Well that fat bitch needed to lose weight. Now her heads half gone she'll probably get a gold star from Weight Watchers."

The men laughed along with the flippant comments that were bantered around while they waited for a truck of back up troops to arrive so they could move onto their next target.

Kenny didn't laugh and joke with the others. He walked over to get an update from his CO and Sgt to see where the next target was. Sgt Brian Davies was stood with the boss Lt Tracey Briar. They looked very similar and people would often comment that their mothers had obviously being putting it around a bit; typical Army banter which didn't offend in most cases. Lt Briar was a handsome man of around 5 ft 10 inches tall with chiselled cheek bones and green eyes and was well built. No one mocked his name after the stories got around of what he had done to the last guy who'd taunted him.

A Sgt from the Royal Green Jackets had passed comment after a drink one night and Lt Briar beat him within an inch of his life. He wasn't what you could call a boxer- more of a brawler. It was unexpected considering his upbringing in Knightsbridge, London. He was a well educated man from a wealthy family, but had said from a young age that he wanted to jump out of aeroplanes and fight the enemy, just like in the movies.

Kenny spoke first, "Boss what's the brief? What's the ETA on the clean up team?"

"They should arrive in the next five minutes hopefully and then we can get the fuck out of dodge and move onto the next target," said Lt Briar.

"The next village will already know we're coming Boss and will be a lot more prepared. Do we know the strength of the village?" Kenny said, looking a little concerned.

Sgt Davies stepped in, "Your right King, they *will* be expecting us, which is why we're going to drive around them and hit the next village so they think we're coming from both directions. We'll hit them on the way back if we've got enough supplies and ammo left. Oh and King, get that fucking scratch looked at on your face before we move out."

Kenny quickly grabbed a medic and got his cut cleaned up. The medic noticed it was quite deep and applied a couple of sutures and a large square protective cover to hold it together until they got back to base.

"Well they won't see me coming with that thing on my fucking face will they?" he joked, and immediately started to add cam cream to it.

They could hear vehicles approaching and through the haze could make out it was a British Military truck. On arrival 20 men jumped out of the back. They were Grenadier Guards who formed part of the infantry; a tough force whose ability is underestimated by many until they got into battle with them. The Lt spoke briefly to the CO of the Guards, Captain Hoost, and then called his men to get in their trucks and prepare to move. The truck drove at break neck speed over the uneven ground for thirty minutes before they once again de-bussed and got into position for the attack. The attack was lead by 2 section this time, but before they could give the signal all hell broke loose.

Shots were fired and rounds came pouring down on the British platoon. It appeared the enemy was smarter than the boss gave them credit for. Two section was pinned down, but Kenny managed to break away to the left flank with Cpl Moore, Private McMann and Black. They headed around the side of the village looking for the firing positions of the enemy. Kenny saw four main machine gun posts that were each manned by three men. The other militia were simply lying on the ground in a straight line with a box of magazines next to them to ensure they never ran out of ammo. Kenny spoke quietly to his men, "Listen up guys, this is heavy shit and we're about to be in the middle of it. I say fuck tactics- let's just run at the bastards and let rip. This should give the boss and the others a chance to get off their fat arses and back in the war. Any questions?"

No-one verbally replied, but they nodded and got to their positions. Black and Moore were going to provide covering fire for King and McMann as they charged the enemy in the hope of causing a diversion and hopefully taking out their gunners. Kenny was a trained sniper, a fantastic shot, so he didn't intend on missing the target. He wanted those gunners; take them out and the enemy would start to crumble and lose confidence. "Go, Go, Go!" whispered Kenny as he went over the top.

They ran at full speed towards the enemy position some 100 yards away. McMann was hitting the guys lying down in a line and laughing to himself at how stupid they were and how easy it was for him to kill them. He fired three shots into each man as he ran towards them.

Seeing this manoeuvre the boss called to his men, "On my command we're going over the top and gonna tear these fuckers apart."

Kenny got to the first machine gun post in seconds. He threw a grenade in which took care of two of them instantly. He fired two rounds into the soldier who was ensuring their supplies were kept topped up. The rounds hit him in the face blowing the back of his head clean off before he put two rounds into the heads of the other men to make sure they were dead.

He charged on firing with incredible accuracy taking out four enemy soldiers lying on the ground. The next machine gunner was now firing in Kenny's direction. Rounds whizzed past him as he carried on running towards the position, he raised his rifle and shot the gunner in the chest sending him and the gun hurtling back. Kenny's heart was pounding; for a moment he really thought his time was up.

Lt Briar screamed at the men to attack. They sprinted towards the enemy who had already started to flee. Private Steve Brice of 2 section took out one of the machine gun posts with his UGL and finished them off with a spray of small arms fire. After running behind the post, he felt a sharp pain in his torso and suddenly he was looking up at the sky, wondering what had just happened.

The battle raged on around him and Lance Cpl David Stone ran to his aid. He grabbed a battle dressing from Brice's combat jacket and ripped his clothes to gain access to the wounded area. The hole was no bigger than a five pence piece in the stomach. He placed the dressing over it and applied pressure.

"Bricey I need you to stay with me mate, everything's gonna be okay. Where does is hurt other than your stomach?" said Stone, trying to keep his friend conscious.

"My back feels kind of weird and I can't feel my legs!" he screamed. "My fucking legs!"

"Calm down mate, we're going to get you out of here and back to base where the Docs will sort you out. You'll be back on your feet causing havoc in no time."

But as he turned him over to see the exit wound, it wasn't good news. The round had gone through his body, splitting his spine. There was bone protruding from his back and clear fluid spilling out. He called for backup but the battle was still going on around them and the Paras were taking heavy fire and other casualties. Brice's eyes rolled and he slipped in and out of consciousness. Stone knew his friend didn't have much time and he could do nothing for him. Two enemy soldiers ran around the corner of a hut and saw Stone tending his wounded colleague. At the same time Stone noticed them and grabbed his rifle. He fired a full magazine of thirty rounds at their location, thankfully hitting both men before they could hit him. Rounds bounced in the dirt all around his position. He leapt to his feet and called out to the others.

"I've got skinny's over here, they're trying to out flank us to the right!" he yelled.

Kenny and McMann heard this and ran over to assist. As McMann ran dodging bullets he caught sight of the enemy coming up behind the large building.

"Fuck me Kenny there must be twenty plus of the bastards round here."

Kenny shouted to the Lt to provide support. The Lt ordered his men to change positions and focus on the large group while leaving four men from 2 section at the rear to ensure they didn't out flank them again. Lance Cpl Stone had taken up a firing position on the corner of the building and was putting down a few rounds at a time to keep their heads down and to make them aware that they knew they were coming. As the team ran forward and got into their places Sgt Robert Blades of 2 section noticed a man lying on the ground. To his horror he realised it was one of his own; he quickly ran to Brice's side and felt for a pulse. There was nothing. He had died quietly on the ground in a

tiny village with no name, fighting for his country and his friends. As Stone turned to take cover he saw the Sgt kneeling by Brice's side and ran over.
"Fuck! Fuck! Fuck! Is he still with us?" he shouted as he approached.

He dropped down to check but Sgt Blades grabbed his hand.
"He's gone. Now get back to your post and drop these fuckers."

There was rage in his eyes as he got to his feet, grabbing his Minimi Light Machine Gun (LMG). He had no intention of letting the death of one of his boys go unpunished but his next action left a look of shock, horror and amazement on the men around him. He ran around the building and when he got to the corner, he didn't stop to check it was clear or safe. He ran straight at the enemy, screaming his war cry as he let loose with a 100 round bag of ammo attached to his LMG. He fired from the hip which wasn't the best position for accuracy, but his marksmanship wasn't on his mind right now. Killing was! Blades was a monster of a man; over 6 feet tall and built like a tank; his brown eyes were wide and round like saucers.

The enemy couldn't believe their eyes; they didn't shoot at him at first they simply watched as he single handily attacked. No back up or support. It was a suicidal action and he should have never survived it, but somehow, miraculously he did. He was unscathed. He took down around ten men before they fired back.

Seeing this act of craziness the Lt ordered his men to provide covering fire and shouted to King and Davies to get him back. They ran around the next hut to the left of the main building and as Kenny popped his head round the corner he came face to face with a huge black man; a member of the militia who with three others was about to do the same thing as Kenny and Davies. They both got a shock, but it was Kenny who struck first. He slammed the butt of his rifle into the man's solar plexus knocking the wind out of him. As he bent over with the pain, Kenny now in a panicked frenzy, quickly stepped around the corner, lifted his rifle, moved the safety catch to automatic and fired at the four men.

The giant he struck took two rounds in the shoulder which of course didn't stop him. He pulled out his knife and lunged at Kenny. Davies who was close behind Kenny turned the corner just in time to put two rounds in the back of his head, dropping him to the floor while his knife sliced through Kenny's trouser leg, just missing the flesh. The other three men didn't get to fire their weapons before they met their end. Kenny and Davies stopped for a moment before bursting into nervous laughter.

"How fucked up was that?" said Kenny.

"Where the hell did they come from?" responded Sgt Davies.

"I just popped my head around for a sneaky peak and his nose was practically against mine. I think I've shit myself," he laughed.

"Right mate, are you good to carry on or has the twat caught you with that blade?"

Kenny looked down and said, "No mate I'm good, but I thought I was going to lose my balls for a second."

"Right then, let's get back to it," Sgt Davies commanded and they jogged to the end of the hut.

This time Kenny looked back at Davies and smiled before popping his head around the corner. They could see Sgt Blades running around like a mad man shouting his war cry as he massacred the enemy soldiers. Kenny and Davies ran towards him shooting three enemy soldiers as they went. When they got within twenty yards of him Kenny shouted to him to warn him of their presence.

"Bob," shouted Kenny, "its Kenny and Bri so don't fucking shoot us."

Sgt Blades turned and looked at them. Rage was still in his eyes and he was oblivious to the carnage around him. Single handed he had killed fifteen enemy militia and wounded another five; the total number of enemy dead was in excess of sixty men. The village was well prepared and had called in men from the neighbouring areas. There were fifteen prisoners who were lined up against a wall of the main building.

Inside the building Lt Briar discovered the

reason why so much effort had been put into defending this tiny unnamed village. He had found hundreds of weapons, mainly Russian, but the most alarming thing was that they were all fairly new. These weren't the cheap throw away weapons that are sold to third world countries and the amount of ammo was staggering.

"Call in the Engineers and let's get this place under guard until we've secured the area," the Lt said to Cpl Moore.

"Yes boss," he replied before crouching on the ground and taking the radio out of his Bergen.

He called in and they sent a team out immediately via Chinook to speed up the process. They couldn't afford for these weapons to fall into the enemies hands. Some of the men had gathered inside the building hoping to escape the soaring heat, some sat down against a wall chilling out while others looked around the rooms to see if any other useful information could be found. The back was of the first room wreaked of urine; it had obviously been used as a latrine by the enemy at some point. The British had no idea how well organised and equipped General Gooder's army was.

The sound of machine gun fire broke the relative peace as a second wave of enemy attacked the village in an attempt to take back what was theirs. It was a short lived rest for the men of 2 Para. The men quickly grabbed their gear and charged out into the open to once again fight for their lives.

Around fifteen enemy soldiers were spotted; they were split into teams of three men and armed with American M16 rifles. The sound was unmistakable to the British and this worried them even more. Just how many weapons did these guys have and what strength was coming next?

Kenny was stood with McMann and Black when it all kicked off again. They grabbed their gear and went for the big building. Kenny did his usual job of kicking in the locked front door and they went from room to room in quick succession clearing it in text book fashion.

When they got to the top floor they grabbed a ladder which was lying on the ground. It was an old home-made ladder used to access the roof by the look of it. Black grabbed the ladder and put it to the skylight and held it in place while Kenny and McMann climbed up onto the roof and set up their firing positions. Black followed. He ran while crouching down to the corner of the roof and set up his position with the LSW.

McMann was the first to make contact. He had removed a brick from the wall around the roof. The wall was a foot high so gave them a reasonable amount of cover in the lying or sitting positions. McMann saw a three man team attempting to sneak around the flank; he lay down and changed the distance on his SUSAT (Sight

Unit Small Arms Trilux) to 300 metres. He breathed slowly and deliberately in and out, second breath in and slowly out again and on the third breath as he began to exhale he held his breath and took the shot. By the time the enemy knew what was happening McMann was on them. His first shot hit the leading soldier in his right eye taking off the side of his head. There was no time to repeat the three breath system. He took the second man down with a shot to his chest and as the third started to make a run for it McMann shot him in between his shoulder blades as he turned to make his escape.

Kenny had brought a Gimpy to the roof so they had awesome fire power, the GPMG was effective up to 800 metres, a thousand in the right hands and today they were most definitely in the right hands. Kenny and Black spotted the other four teams spread out across the Northern end of the village. Kenny took aim through the iron sight and started firing in small bursts of around five rounds at a time. Black opened up seconds later taking out a whole three man team in the first couple of minutes of the battle and Kenny had either killed or injured another eight men.

The militia knew their fate now and so the remaining uninjured man decided to try a new tact. He lay in the dead ground for cover while he gathered his thoughts; he took a picture of his wife and three children from his chest pocket and kissed them goodbye; a tear ran down his face before he made the brave move to crawl over to his comrades.

McMann noticed he was gathering grenades from his dead and injured colleagues and attaching them to his webbing across his waist and chest.

"Kenny mate, it looks like we've got ourselves a suicide bomber in the wings," said McMann.

"Cheers bud, we need to stop this fucker before he gets near the lads. Black, get on comms and tell the boss to move back until we've got him," Kenny said assertively.

Black set about getting in touch with Lt Briar and shouted back to Kenny.

"I'm on it dude!"

This set both Kenny and McMann off laughing.

"What the fuck is with the Teenage Mutant Ninja Turtle talk you dick head?" said Kenny ridiculing his best friend.

The bomber on the ground stood up in full view and started running towards the men screaming at the top of his lungs. Kenny took aim and let off a belt of around 100 rounds of 7.62mm. As it hit him in the chest, the moving bomb exploded. Private Bob Newland and Private Matt Hands had stood up to take the shot when Kenny struck the victim; the blast hit the men knocking them off their feet. Newland jumped back up as quickly as he went down but Hands was down for a minute longer as he lay there thinking how lucky he was.

Lt Briar called the rest of the team to clear the area and take care of any injured enemy so they could be questioned if necessary. Two section was given this task and so Sgt Blades took the lead. His men were a little weary after seeing his reaction earlier but were glad he was on their side.

They found five injured and three close to death. Private Spence shot one man in the head then turned and killed the other man lying close behind him, with two shots in the chest before walking over to another area to search for survivors. He heard another shot to his left. It was Blades; he took it upon himself to ensure the last dying man got his wish. He shot him three times in the chest and sent the man to his God. The injured were given medical attention and then moved to the other side of the village to await the next Heli to arrive.

Chapter 2

The engineers arrived at long last, taking over the munitions found in the building. The Para's climbed aboard a Chinook which followed the engineer's heli; it took them back to base to gather their things together and get ready for a night mission. The second village they attacked had taken longer than expected so the attacks on the other villages were cancelled. The truck they came in stayed with the engineers to assist.

As soon as they got back to camp, Kenny and Black dropped their kit and went to the shower block to clean up. Kenny felt exhausted; it had been a busy day so far and a long one at that but he knew he had to shake it off, as he had done many times before, in order to get the job done.

He stood in the shower and let the water cascade off him; his eyes were closed as he relaxed, flashing the 2 Para tattoo on his upper right arm and a huge tattoo on his back of a Gargoyle, wearing the red beret of the Parachute Regiment. His arms were huge and vascular and covered in small scars from close calls in battle or simply throwing himself around. His waist was thick, yet he had a faint outline of a six pack underneath his mass. His thighs were the envy of many a soldier in the Regiment; all twenty-eight inches of them. He was a keen rugby player who loved to TAB (Tactical Advance to Battle – the army's name for moving at speed carrying a heavy Bergen). This was Kenny's thing, and he was damn good at it; his 18 inch calves were equally as impressive. Kenny was *not* a man to be tangled with.

After the shower Kenny and Black headed back to the sleeping area to get their heads down. Kenny walked in through the tent door and saw most of 3 section lying fast asleep, when he heard a voice shouting his name from outside the tent.

"Cpl King, can you come here please?" called the officer.

Kenny walked back outside into the sun and went over to the officer whose voice he recognised.

"Yes Sir, what can I do for you?" he asked politely, when all he wanted to do was get some food down him and then a couple of hours sleep in preparation for the night mission.

"Cpl I don't know what your guys think they're doing or who the hell they think they are but I demand some order. Three of them walked past me earlier and failed to salute."

Kenny was furious, "Are you fucking kidding me Sir!" he said in a raised voice. "We've been on Ops for days, we're wiped out. They probably didn't even see you; they wouldn't deliberately ignore an officer Sir."

The officer was startled by Kings reaction, "Do you know who I am Cpl?" asked the officer.

"Yes sir I recognise you, but your name escapes me. We served in Northern Ireland together didn't we?" Kenny asked, hoping he would give his name.

"I'm Captain Stewart, camp officer on duty and that still doesn't give your men the right to break Army regulations. I want the men shaved and in clean kit ready for inspection in 30 mins Cpl. Is that understood?"

Captain Stewart turned and walked away.

Kenny just stood there, trying to hold back his urge to punch the officer in the face. He stormed over to the command tent, still wearing nothing but a towel, and knocked on the tent door before entering. The atmosphere is the tent was hectic and thick cigarette smoke lingered in the air. The occupants took one look at him and stared at the half naked man standing before them.

Kenny called across to his senior officers, "Sir, can I have a quick word? It's quite urgent boss."

Lt Briar and Major Anderson followed Kenny out of the tent. They both had great respect for him, so if he said something was urgent then they believed him.

"What's up King?" asked Lt Briar.

"Sir you know I'm not one to complain and moan about Army politics and all that stuff but I'm fucked off to my back teeth," said Kenny with anger in his voice.

"What the hell happened King?" asked the Major.

Kenny explained the situation, and they were both as furious as Kenny at this officer's petty behaviour. Especially when it was 2 Para going out on missions day and night, taking this war back to General Gooder's men.

"I'll deal with this issue personally Cpl, rest assured. It's better coming from me as a higher rank than from you Tracey," said the Major.

"No problem boss," replied Lt Briar.

Kenny went back to his tent and threw on some clean civi clothes before heading to the mess for his long overdue feed. He ate a huge meal before walking back to the tent and literally collapsing onto his bed.

***

The alarm went off and it was time to get ready for the next mission.

Kenny climbed out of bed, got his camouflage uniform on and went out to grab more food before they headed out. He sat with his section eating a chicken dinner followed by rhubarb crumble with custard. Black was at the end of the table with McMann and Cassum. They all bantered as they sat eating their meal and McMann shouted across the table to Kenny.

"Hey King! Dude, what's happening with you," putting on a surfer dude voice and the whole table burst into fits of laughter.

"Ha fucking ha! You're a bunch of bastards do

you know that? I can't help what comes out in the midst of a battle you set of twats." Black said in a raised voice.

His Scottish accent was always stronger when he was angry.

Kenny looked over laughing at his friend, "Oh come on Rich, it was fucking funny. I ask you to get on the blower to the boss and you call me dude, I mean what the *fuck* is all that about? What a twat!"

Kenny decided it best to leave their conversation there and fill up for the mission ahead. He stared down at his plate, and said nothing more until his plate was clean and his belly full.

Chapter 3

They stood at the heli pad awaiting the next order. Lt Briar walked over to them with Major Anderson and accompanying the officers was Captain Stewart.

"Heads up Kenny, it's Captain America and he looks pissed," said Sgt Davies.

The Major took up the stance in front of the men and delivered the operational details, and when he was done he called Kenny over for a word.

"Cpl King, Captain Steward would like a chat with you in our presence if that's okay? I don't want this to look any worse than it already is."

"No problem with me boss, what can I do for you this evening *Sir*?" asked Kenny, rather sarcastically.

He thought he was about to get a roasting from the officers.

"Cpl I apologise for earlier, maybe I was being a little petty considering how hard your team had been working," said the Captain.

"Okay Sir not to worry. What's done is done and I have no problem with you as an individual or an officer. I enjoyed working with you back in Ireland."

"Good Cpl I'm glad to hear it; however what I won't tolerate is having my orders questioned and then running off to your boss to get me a bollocking. Is that understood?" the Captain said in a forceful tone.

Major Anderson was looking on at Kenny with a smirk on his face when he spoke next.

"Well I'm glad your enjoyed working together because Captain Stewart is going operational with you lot tonight."

"Yes Sir," responded King in a respectful manner.

"Right Sir, what's the plan for the evening?"

The Captain looked on at him and smiled. He knew King was a cracking Corporal who would carry out *any* order given to him without question and who never failed to deliver an objective.

"Lt Briar will be leading 2 section for the remainder of the tour and you have the pleasure of me. Tonight's operation will kick off at 2300 hours on the airfield. We will be taken in by Chinook as a full platoon and dropped at three separate locations in Algeria. All you need to know is that we will be hitting a heavily fortified compound which intelligence informs us is a training ground for General Gooder's soldiers."

"Do we know what strength and weapons they have?"

"Intel reckons around 200 men and weapons vary from AK's to M16's and mortars to LAW's (Light Anti-tank weapon). They spotted at least 30 officers amongst the ranks; they liked to show their authority when wandering around camp apparently."

"How good is the intel Sir?" asked Kenny

wondering if they were committing suicide on this mission.

"It's as good as it gets Corporal," snapped the Captain. "This is British intel. The boys in SF saw it themselves and fed it back to base less than an hour ago. Is that good enough for you Corporal?"

"Yes Sir, it wasn't meant disrespectfully but we've had some shit intel since we got here. No offence Sir."

"Okay King so long as we know where we stand. I don't want, and won't take, any shit from you nor anyone else. Let's get the men together and get them loaded up. You've got fifteen minutes to get them to the pad. As you were," said the Captain, ending the conversation.

Kenny jogged over to the tent and called the men together, explaining the detail for the evening but doing so without telling them the expected strength of the enemy. Although many of the men would relish the thought of fighting against such a force, many of the younger less experienced soldiers probably wouldn't.

All three sections of Reconnaissance Platoon got into their positions in the Chinook; one section situated at the back nearest the tailgate as they would be dropped first some 4 km inside Algeria, then two section who would be dropped a further 2 km North and finally three section who would be dropped 4 km's North again. This mission was an in and out job. It was hitting the enemy hard on their own turf and then retreating several miles back to the relative safety of the Algerian border to the South of the country, to a small area called Tinzaouten.

The metal floor was cold so the men sat on their Bergen's; there was no point in trying to hold a conversation as the noise from the rotors was deafening. The Chinook had been stripped of any creature comforts to allow maximum space inside so they could deploy mobility troops from both Pathfinder Platoon and the SAS.

The Chinook dropped all three sections without a hiccup before heading back to base in Niger. The teams each had their own objective which the others knew nothing about. It was 2 section who reached its objective first. They had tabbed 1 km to an airfield which housed a communication tower. The base was practically deserted with only 12 men in total at the site. Eight of these were signals personnel and the other four were foot soldiers in General Gooder's militia. Lt Briar got his men into position ensuring everyone knew their job and the escape route along with emergency RV.

Cpl Stevens got into position behind the main comms room door with Privates Spence and Hand (who everyone called panda due to the black rings under his eyes) as his team. Cpl Bands and Private Newland had Lance Cpl Stollers in their team of three at the entrance to the accommodation block, while Lt Briar and Sgt Blades stayed back in an OP in case anything went wrong.

Stevens and Bands looked at each other across a patch of pot holed tarmac and gave each other three nods. After the third nod of the head the two Cpls kicked the entrance doors in simultaneously throwing in a flash bang grenade (white phosphorus) to disorientate the enemy before running into the rooms firing at anything that moved. Cpl Stevens shot two of the foot soldiers as he entered the room and the other two men came under the same fate when Spence put two rounds in each of the enemy's heads, before clearing the rest of the building. While Panda watched the door, he was disappointed he didn't get to kill anyone but the night was still young and anything could happen.

Cpl Bands and his team ran through the accommodation block at high speed killing the two soldiers and three of the signals men. One of the men was taking a shower in the furthest part of the block when the assault began. Hearing the commotion he decided it would be easier to surrender than put up a fight. Unfortunately for him the Paras weren't there to take prisoners. But Bands took his prisoner to the control room and asked were all the comms lines were situated. Sgt Blades went in to see what was going on while the Lt kept watch; the signalman didn't know what was coming when the Sgt arrived. He thought the superior would ensure his safety.

The captor was being questioned by Cpl Bands as Sgt Blades looked on impatiently. They all knew that they had to blow the comms and get out of there as soon as possible. The man told Cpl Bands he didn't know where the main comms line was situated on the base. Blades had had enough and smashed his fist into the man's face breaking his nose, the force of the blow jarring his head back violently.

"You've got ten fucking seconds to tell us what we want to know or I'll fucking finish you here and now!" screamed Blades.

His eyes said it all, he was furious and in no mood to mess around.

"I don't know," cried the man in broken English.

"Five seconds," Blades said calmly.

The man looked at him with absolute terror in his eyes. Blades picked up his rifle and aimed it at the man's shoulder.

"I'm not going to ask again," he said.

"I......."

His voice trailed off before letting out a scream as the first bullet ripped through his right shoulder, shattering his shoulder blade. The other Paratroopers were shocked but knew better than to question Sgt Blades when in a rage.

"Last fucking chance Abdul," he called one more time.

He looked at the Sgt, speechless and truly terrified. The Sgt raised his rifle again, only this time he aimed higher and fired two rounds into the man's face, blowing off the back of his head. He hit the deck and was surrounded in a pool of blood. "Right, get the fucking explosives in place and let's get it done," he ordered, emotionless.

Lt Briar came into the room and saw the body on the ground; he simply passed it a glance and casually walked past before speaking to the Sgt.

"We need to move sharpish Sgt. We've got a lot of ground to cover and we only have five more hours of daylight."

"Yes boss, we're on it," he responded, while watching his men move into action laying the detonation charges.

The team placed the charges and moved to a safe location before setting off the controlled explosion. Within minutes Sirens could be heard in the distance and they knew a unit of General Gooder's men would be dispatched to investigate and prepared to fight. Lt Briar led the men across country. The Paras were no strangers to tabbing with full kit in just about any terrain, but this time they knew they had a hostile force hot on their tails.

In the mean time 1 section had also reached its objective. A high priority operative needed to be kidnapped and taken back to the base in Niger. This wasn't such an easy task. The snatch itself went without a hitch but getting the man to move at speed with the team was a whole different ball game. He was 5ft 11 inches tall and weighed around 14 stone, a heavy smoker who coughed constantly. This didn't stop the man from smoking an average of sixty cigarettes a day.

After struggling with the man for the first kilometre, Cpl Steve Taylor had had enough and smacked him in the head with the butt of his SA80 rifle, knocking him unconscious. This meant they had to carry him the remaining 3 km, which the others weren't too pleased about. The four privates who were given this task were forced to see it as a challenge, just like test week on P Company in basic training and they seemed to enjoy it. There was no-one chasing 1 section as it would be a while before anyone noticed the Algerian man was missing.

It was 0100 hours when 3 section arrived at the enemy training ground and began their reconnaissance. Sgt Davies took Black, McMann and Lance Cpl Stone with him to the East side of the camp and cut through the fence at ground level, slipping undetected into the compound while Captain Stewart took King, Cassum and Moore to the South to where the entrance to the camp was situated.

They watched for fifteen minutes, observing enemy numbers and movements. This wasn't as long as they had hoped for but time was against them, and they had 10 kilometers to cover under the black canvas of the night sky. This was potentially with the rest of General Gooder's militia after them once they had completed their hit and run mission. Sgt Davies and his team laid down several claymore mines with trip wires outside the doors to the main accommodation block, which they believed was home to some 200 trainees.

Meanwhile Captain Stewart and his team were getting ready to put in a full blown assault on the main gate. The gate had two machine gun posts, one at ground level to the right of the gate and a second to the left, situated three metres up in a small tower. Each position had two men in it and the gate itself was manned by four more guards, all armed with AK47 assault rifles. The machine gunners were armed with soviet 7.62 mm Pecheneg machine guns (PMG's).

Kenny and the Captain got into position 200 metres directly in front of the gateway in some shrub and on Captain Stewarts command Kenny would unleash all hell as he opened up with his Minimi LMG. Cassum and Moore would wait until the gunners gave their full attention to Kenny and the Captain, before simultaneously firing their 66mm LAW's into both machine gun positions.

The Captain looked at Kenny with a nervous tension.

"Good luck King, whenever you're ready let's give them some."

Kenny squeezed the trigger of his Minimi and immediately took out two of the men on the gate with his accurate shooting. All hell broke loose with both machine gunners firing everything they had in Kenny's direction. As they did this Cassum and Moore fired the LAW's into the positions blowing them apart killing all four men; Captain Stewart didn't want to miss out on the action and so got up and ran towards the gate screaming his war cry at the top of his lungs. "Attack!!!"

The whole camp woke up and sentries came running from all over the compound, shooting as they ran towards the entrance. Panic struck the enemy soldiers as they struggled to understand what had happened or who was attacking them at their strong hold. A senior officer in the militia shouted commands to his men to set up all round defences on the camp and to sound the alarm. As one of the soldiers ran towards the weapon stores he tripped one of the claymore mines blowing him clear across the yard and lay there with his left arm hanging on by a few strands of skin, screaming for help; his body was riddled with puncture holes from the ball bearings that were spewed out of the mine. The accommodation block emptied at great speed running straight into the Para's trap, blowing up dozens of them as they exited the building. The building caught fire and was filling the bedrooms with thick black smoke as the fire spread through the lower floor.

Sgt Davies then let rip with his SA80 and the others followed suit, firing at the enemy killing dozens of militia as they scattered out of control, some of which hadn't even got to their weapons and so couldn't put up a fight against the Paras offensive.

Black was carrying the Gimpy and was cutting men down left, right and centre. McMann fired the NLAW (Next Generation Light Anti-tank weapon) at a tank as the crew ran towards it, taking out one of its tracks and putting a hole in the front of the vehicle, making it vulnerable to mines and low level small arms fire.

Once the tank was hit Sgt Davies called to his men.

"Right lads fall back and give covering fire as you go. We don't want these fuckers shooting us in the back. If you get split up we'll meet up at the RV in one hour. Don't be late!"

Kenny was providing covering fire for the Captain who had clearly got visions of valour in his mind. Kenny was furious at the Captain and shouted for him to get back into cover but he couldn't hear his call. He continued forward without any consideration for his own or anyone else's safety. Forward he ran, firing wildly at the enemy. Cassum tried calling to the officer but all he got was a crazed reply.

"Come on men follow me into glory!"

Seconds later Captain Stewart fell to the ground as dozens of rounds sliced through his body. A machine gun post had been set up at the corner of one of the buildings and as he ran forward without backup from his men he was cut down- killed in action (KIA). He was thirty years old and had served in the Parachute Regiment for nine years. Six years with 1 Para and the last three with 2 Para's Charlie Company before being posted to Recce Platoon for two days before being killed. Kenny couldn't get to the Capt to recover his body so ordered his men to shoot and scoot which meant running back into cover firing at random to keep the enemy guessing; manoeuvring from side to side to avoid getting hit by the wave of munitions being fired in their general direction.

Luckily for them the enemy weren't very accurate and were *still* trying to figure out what the hell was happening.

The RV was 800 metres due East with an emergency RV a further 800 metres South of this. Kenny, Cassum and Cpl Moore made it to the RV in just four minutes which was pretty good going considering the amount of ammo they were carrying. Sgt Davies, Black and McMann came in shortly after, trailing behind came Lance Cpl Stone who was limping as he arrived. With the enemy hot on their heels they didn't have time to stop and discuss things in depth, but Sgt Davies noticed the obvious.

"Where the fuck is the boss?" he yelled.

"Dead mate," responded Kenny.

"How? I mean, what happened?"

"Does it fucking matter Bri? Let's just keep every fucker else alive and we'll discuss the details when we're safe behind our own lines," Kenny said with urgency in his voice.

The seven men tabbed through the woodland stopping occasionally to check behind them. Stone was struggling with the pace and Kenny was getting worried about him.

"What's wrong Dave? Have you sprained something? Coz we really need to get a fucking wiggle on mate," quizzed Kenny.

Stone looked a grey colour as he stopped for a moment to get his breath and answer Kenny's questions.

"I've been hit mate. I don't want to look coz that might make me worse but my arse and left thigh are fucking killing me. I can't move any faster Kenny, I'm sorry mate I just can't."

Kenny's face dropped and he felt a surge of guilt for not asking when he saw Stone at the first RV. Sgt Davies stopped and grabbed his first aid kit from his Bergen.

"Let's have a look," said the Sgt, stopping to inspect the wounded man.

He got down onto his knees and asked Stone to lie down while he looked at it. Stone lay face down and was shaking with the pain. He had in fact been shot twice, once in the left buttock and again in the left thigh.   The thigh was a clean shot which fortunately for him had gone straight through, but it was bleeding badly. Sgt Davies couldn't remove the bullet from his buttock but managed to stop the bleeding at least for the moment, but they all knew that it would start again once he began to run. They had only been going for 2 km and with another eight to go they were seriously worried about Stone.

McMann, who was also a trained medic, came over and looked at the wound before speaking to Stone.

"Listen Dave I know you're in a lot of pain but we've got 8 clicks to do in the next 90 minutes so I need you to pretend you're on selection for the SAS and give it 100%."

He let out a roar and shook himself off as he got up.

"Your right mate, I'm a fucking Para and one day I'll be a SF trooper so I better get the fuck on with it."

Kenny smiled at the motivational speech McMann had given his friend. They started running only this time they couldn't afford to go at tabbing pace which averaged around 11 minute miles. It was an all out run as fast as possible to make it to the safe RV over the border and into Niger. Kenny led the way and Davies took up the rear position making sure Stone didn't fall behind or lose the rest of the team.

The enemy was closing fast and they had sent out choppers with eight man teams armed to the back teeth, as well as truck loads of men along the main routes. Kenny came across a main road and realised there was no way around it.

"We're gonna have to make a dash for it lads and hope they aren't watching this road."

Kenny and McMann made it across, then Black and Stone. As Cpl Moore stood up to run, head lights appeared over the crest of a hill on the road catching him in its full beam. The truck increased speed as the driver saw him and blazed his horn to notify the men that he'd spotted someone. Moore raised his SA80 rifle and set it to automatic; he fired a full thirty round magazine in the direction of the vehicle. Davies and King both fired at the main body of the truck as it approached, seeing blood spray upwards in the early morning sky. The truck stopped and the remaining men jumped out and began firing at Moore and both sides of the road.

Kenny had to keep his men moving, "Stone, you keep going mate and we'll catch you up."

"I can fight mate, your gonna fucking need me by the looks of it," responded Stone.

"I know you can fight but I need to keep you alive so cut the shit and fucking move. We'll catch you up, now fuck off!"

Cpl Moore kept pouring fire onto the vehicle whilst McMann and Stone took off to make it to the emergency RV. McMann struggled with the act of leaving his friends behind in a heavy fire fight. He knew that Kenny sent him with Stone to make sure he survived; he wasn't sure Stone's act of positivity would last if he was on his own. At least this way he would probably want to keep up the act as he wouldn't want to lose face in front of his mates.

Kenny and Black moved forward up the left flank and put covering fire down to ensure their colleagues made it across the road and on to the ERV. An enemy soldier ran around from behind the truck with an American M60 GPMG and put heavy fire down onto the team crossing the road. They were all across bar Sgt Davies who was firing accurately hitting enemy soldiers as they ran forward to fight. At one point he laughed out loud and shouted to Kenny.
"Hey Kenny this is like that game......Lemons int it. They just keep lining themselves up for the fucking kill."

Kenny saw the gunner's shots getting closer to Davies and so picked himself up from a lying position, putting himself at great risk. He raised his Minimi and fired around twenty rounds into the enemy, killing him. He then ran towards the truck and threw two grenades over the top, exploding behind the vehicle and killing another four and forcing them to retreat. Davies moved across the road and shouted for Kenny to move.

Kenny and Black moved back and followed their friends to the ERV. They ran at a phenomenal pace to ensure they didn't get left behind; all three of them were ultra fit so it wasn't surprising that they covered the remaining six kilometres in twenty five minutes. As they approached the ERV they could see a group of armed men waiting in the exact spot that they were to be picked up. The men didn't look British or American so they thought something was up and had to think fast on their feet. Stone had lost a lot of blood and was now slipping in and out of consciousness. McMann got a drip and pushed the needle into his friend's left hand and started pumping the fluid into his veins. Within thirty seconds Stone was feeling better as the fluid rushed through his body giving him a sudden surge of life and energy.

The soldiers were carrying AK47's and AK74's but one stood out from the rest as he was carrying an American M16 A2. Could it be the pickup was real and these were the right men? Davies and King pondered for a few minutes before deciding their next plan of action.

"Ok team," said Sgt Davies as he gathered them round for a quick field brief. "Lance Cpl Stone is injured and needs medical attention real fast. So we're going to send him over to see if it's for real and if it goes tits up then we'll let them have it. Are we all clear?" he asked looking around at his team.

They all nodded. They knew Stone had

volunteered for the role of bait and he knew the risks were high, but he was already dying so he figured better they get him than the others. He crawled thirty feet to the right of the Paras position before standing up and limping over to the soldiers. As he approached he made it to within five feet of them before speaking.

"Hi guys, is this the ERV?" Stone asked.

An American man turned around fast and pointed his M16 at him before saying the password.

"Mowgli!"

"Hindi," replied Stone, before falling to his knees.

The strange looking pick up team were in fact the real deal; a team of men who had escaped General Gooder's Army and were now working with the Americans. The American was a US Green Beret, part of the US Army Airborne Special Forces; Sgt First Class (SFC) Mike Heskinski whose parents were of Russian origin. A strange combination for an American of his age, he was 40 years old and had been a soldier for twenty years. This would be his last active duty before being transferred back to Fort Bragg to be an instructor for his last eighteen months of service.

He went by the name Hesk and had seen action in two tours of Vietnam, El Salvador, Panama, Somalia, Iraq, Afghanistan, and now here in the Horn of Africa. He had a thick Texan accent and looked as tough as they came; standing six feet tall, with a muscular physique and a weathered face and the thousand yard stare.

The pick-up team rushed to Stone's aid before the rest of the section got up exposing their position and jogging over to the ERV. Sgt Davies introduced himself to Hesk.

"Hi, I'm glad you were the bloody pick-up team. I'm Sgt Davies of 2 Para."

"Good morning Sgt," he responded with his thick Texan twang. "You guys look like hell, we better get moving before the skinny's catch us up."

He spoke to his team in African and they put Stone on a stretcher and put an IV in his arm as the remainder of 3 section climbed aboard the truck. They were taken to a small airfield where a Sea King helicopter awaited them. As they arrived they noticed some of the men standing around smoking. It was Lt Briar with Cpl's Bands and Stevens. Kenny looked oddly at the Lt as he knew the boss didn't usually smoke and wondered if their operation had gone so badly that he felt the need for a cigarette.

Briar and his team had been at the initial RV on time and so had been transferred to the airstrip to await the other sections. They had been there for approximately thirty minutes which had given Briar time to start thinking about what had gone on back in the comms room. Sgt Blades actions were beginning to concern him and he could sense that the men were becoming uneasy around him, not knowing what to say to him or how to act for fear of him losing his temper.

Kenny walked over to the three of them speaking as he approached.

"Bloody hell boss it must have been bad if you've taken to the death sticks."

"Don't ask Kenny," Briar responded clearly, struggling with his thoughts.

He knew the right thing to do would be to have Blades arrested as soon as they got back to camp and have the military psychologist to take a look at him to see if he was still fit for duty. Kenny could see that Bands also looked very uncomfortable with the conversation. Stevens said nothing.

Sgt Blades was talking to Sgt Davies and SFC Hesk about the operation and how he didn't rate Sgt Fisher of 1 section.

"He's a fucking liability I tell ya," Blades said.

"He's only been with 2 Para for six months and they give him a fucking Recce Squad. I've been with 2 Para for six fucking years and haven't had a squad for 12 months coz of fucking newbie's like him coming in and brown nosing the CO."

"Okay Bob, simmer down mate. Let it go, okay." Davies said in a calm flat voice.

Hesk piped up saying, "I got to tell you man, I don't agree with bad mouthing one of your own. Where I come from we all stick together or the machine starts to fall apart."

He was clearly disappointed with Blades comment and didn't want to take part in the conversation.

"One of fucking us!" Blades retaliated, "He's a hat, just in from the fucking airy fairy Rifles Regiment."

Cpl Taylor of 1 section over heard the conversation and went over to speak to Sgt Fisher.

"Bill, I'm not trying to stir the shit but that prick Blades is over there slagging you off."

Fisher listened to Taylor and looked over at Blades and the others before responding.

"Thanks Steve but I'm not gonna waste my time on that fucker, especially at the minute while he's on a death wish. Now I'm not being a chicken shit or anything but he's on the edge at the minute and I for one don't wanna be around him when he goes. Do you?"

"No, I suppose not. He's a nut job, but I thought you should know all the same. Oh I have to say that Davies was telling him to shut the fuck up and the Yank was telling him he was out of order for talking smack about you."

"Glad to hear that, at least I know there are still some decent blokes around," he gathered his gear together ready to load into the chopper while his men did the same.

They arrived back at base camp and all NCO's and Officers went immediately into debrief accompanied by Hesk. They shuffled into the large air conditioned tent where Capt Silvers stood at the front with a large white projector screen

57

behind him. He loaded the images up from the cameras used by each section and Lt Briar gave a brief explanation as to what his section found at the comms station. He didn't mentioned the torture and murder of the enemy soldier as he still wasn't sure how to tackle it but he knew he needed to talk to Silvers ASAP.

Sgt Davies and Sgt Fisher then got up and explained their individual operations; Fisher had lead a text book assault which impressed almost everyone in the tent. Sgt Blades looked on in disgust as Fisher received high praise from the CO and the Lt. He clearly didn't like Fisher due to the fact he came from a crap hat regiment into his beloved Parachute Regiment despite Fisher having completed the All Arms Para course some five years previous.

After the brief was over Capt Silvers sensing something wasn't quite right with Lt Briar asked him to stay back for an Officers brief. Once everyone else had left the tent he spoke with concern to Briar.

"So Tracey are you going to tell me what's up?"

"Oh Sir, I don't know where to start. I really don't want to be seen as a weak leader but I can't ignore what happened in the comms room tonight. I found a dead soldier on the ground, his hands were tied and he'd been shot in the head. It was obvious that this was the work of one of our guys and Sgt Blades was standing over him with a rifle in his hand, so I suspect it was him. Cpl Bands came to see me afterwards and told me what had happened. Apparently Blades roughed the guy up a little before giving him ten seconds to tell him what he knew and he literally gave him ten fucking seconds before he capped him."

Briar was physically shaking as he spoke to the Captain.

"Jesus H Christ Tracey, I'll get the MP's over to his tent now and have him arrested. He needs his fucking head looking at. I know this is a dirty violent war but we can't be just offing the enemy when they have been captured or surrender to us."

He grabbed his phone and called the MP's and explained the situation. Minutes later a Jeep pulled up outside the Sgt's tent and four MP's went in armed to the teeth and ready for a fight. Blades was asleep on his bed when they walked in. The team of military policemen were lead by Sgt Scurr. Scurr knew Blades quite well from his days in Aldershot when Blades was frequently arrested for fighting in the bars in town.

He silently waved motioning the three Cpl's to make their move while he was lying on his left side asleep. Two of them quickly shoved Blades onto his face grabbing his arms behind his back and slapping the handcuffs on him. He immediately woke up and started to struggle, quickly realising it wasn't worth it he gave up the fight and simply accepted that he was in a no win situation. They turned him and stood him up at the side of his bed as Sgt Scurr explained the reason for his arrest. He didn't respond, instead he just walked with the Cpls to the vehicle, climbed inside and was taken away to the jail to await the outcome of an investigation and then his military trial.

It was three days later when Sgt Blades stood before the Battalion CO of 2 Para, Lt Colonel Simpson. Simpson wasn't known for his tolerance of bullish behaviour from his troops and certainly wasn't going to accept it from one of his SNCO's. Due to the serious nature of the offence Simpson court marshalled Blades and sent him back to the UK to stand trial for murder. Robert Blades was sentenced to fifteen years in prison but was found dead in his cell after just two weeks. He had hung himself.

It is a sad fact of life that combat stress contributes to dozens, perhaps even hundreds of suicides every year and yet very little is done about it by the Government; the very Government that sends these young men to war in the first place.

The Recce Platoon continued to be sent out on small hit and run operations over the following month before finally getting a reprieve. They had been in Africa for four months without a recreational break. The word came in from the Lt that they were being flown to Morocco for a week of R&R. The men of 1 and 3 sections would be going, two section had been to Turkey some six weeks earlier for their R&R break and were gutted they weren't getting the chance to go to Morocco.

The troops arrived in Marrakech, Morocco at around 0300 hours local time and headed straight for their rooms. They were two to a room so as usual King and Black bunked together. It was still twenty six degrees despite the time of the morning and the rooms didn't have air conditioning. Black couldn't believe they didn't have it and went back to reception to see if they had a fan that they could hire. Luckily they did and by the time he got back up to the room which was on the 10th floor Kenny was sound asleep snoring heavily.

"Fucking great," Black muttered quietly, watching his friend as he climbed onto his bed some three feet away.

It was 1000 hours before Black woke up; he turned his head to see Kenny lying on his bed looking up at the ceiling.

"Hey big fella," Black said tiredly, "How you doing?"

Kenny sat up on the edge of the bed facing Black.

"Oh man that was one hell of a sleep. I don't think I moved from the spot I lay down in, I can't believe how wrecked I was."

"Well its hardly a surprising is it mate, we been in the shit for four fucking months?"

"Yeah, you got that right brother. So we hitting breakfast before it closes?" Kenny said rubbing his stomach.

Black nodded, got out of bed and threw on some clothes. Kenny grabbed a shower while Black made a coffee. They were on a half board basis but were given apartments with self catering facilities in them. The two men walked into the restaurant and saw eight men sitting in the far corner of the room next to open patio doors, feeling the breeze washing over them as they sat and ate there food. The men acknowledged each other and Kenny and Black went straight to the breakfast bar and filled their plates. There was an attractive Moroccan girl, maybe 20 years old serving behind the counter and she smiled as she looked at what they both had on their plates.

"Four bacon, four sausage, two eggs, beans, tomatoes and three toast each. Wow, I guess you guys are hungry this morning?"

She spoke very good English and smiled as she chatted to them both.

"You aint seen nothing yet sweetheart," came the response from Black. "I'll be back for more; I just didn't want to look greedy."

He laughed as he walked away, and Kenny stood chatting with her for a few minutes before sitting down with the other soldiers. The food wasn't especially hot but every mouthful felt like his taste buds were exploding. It seemed such a long time since he had a good meal, not that the food on camp was bad but he had spent so much time on Op's that he usually missed lunch and dinner and only got breakfast if he could stay awake long enough to make it to the first sitting.

"So what were you and the bint talking about?" asked Black, referring to the girl at the counter.

"Just asking her about the area and where the good pubs are and stuff," he continued to eat.

"Is she up for a fucking shag then do you reckon?"

"Not with you she isn't ya ugly twat," he joked, and the table laughed out loud with other holiday makers looking on at them.

After breakfast they made their way to the pool area and pulled out a row of seventeen sun loungers along the length of the large pool. The pool attendant looked on, not sure of what to do about it and looking at the size and type of men that were doing it he decided it was probably best to leave them well alone. After all they had as much right as anyone else to be there, it was their holiday too despite the fact that the Army was paying for it. Lt Briar came down with 2nd Lieutenant Mellor, a new officer fresh out of Sandhurst. He was a wiry little man of five foot six inches who weighed around nine stone and didn't look like he could fight his way out of a paper bag. But he had passed Para training with relative ease and breezed through Sandhurst passing out with the Sword of Honour award, which goes to the best Officer in training, so he obviously had something about him.

After the introductions they sat at the end

of the row of beds next to King and Black, two at a time the men came to the join the others by the pool with the exception of L Cpl Harrison and Private Bell of 1 section. They both preferred the beach to sitting around a pool all day, plus they figured they might get lucky and meet some female companions while they were there.

Kenny lay on his front, absorbing the thirty degree heat from the sun while he drifted in and out of sleep. He was still recovering from the four months of none stop Op's in Africa and he knew that the week would be over before he knew it and he'd be back into the swing of things for another seven weeks before they would finally be sent back to the UK. Throughout the day pints of larger were brought to the pool by the bar staff and a tab was opened for each room. Kenny got up and dived into the pool which had looked so inviting while he sunbathed. As he hit the water, the cold rush took his breath away and he gasped as he surfaced, much to the amusement of his colleagues.

"Phwoar, it's fucking freezing," he shouted to the other men.

"Ya soft twat, call yourself a fucking paratrooper," came the response from Black.

The banter was repeated by some of the others. Lt Briar and Mellor were discussing each member of the Recce Platoon; Briar knew the new Lt would do a fine job but was concerned that he hadn't done any time with a regular unit before being sent to Recce Platoon. After all, the Recce troops were the toughest in the battalion and required strong experienced leadership if the shit hit the fan, which it did regularly in Africa. Lt Briar had to leave for a telephone meeting with the Brass and left Lt Mellor with the other men. He got up and sat at a table in the shade watching the men he would come to lead on the battlefield at some point in the near future.

He watched Kenny climb out of the pool, heavily muscled with numerous scars on his body. Kenny got dried off and walked over to the table where the Lt was sitting.

"Mind if I join you Sir?" he asked.

"Not at all, Cpl King isn't it?" he asked.

"Yes Sir, but when we're on holiday you can call me Kenny," he smiled at the Lt hoping he would get the point that he was not a soldier for this week but a tourist on holiday enjoying the Moroccan sun.

"Fair enough," the Lt responded smiling and laughing slightly, "So, *Kenny*, I hear good things about you from Lt Briar, oops sorry, I mean Tracey."

Kenny laughed at the awkwardness of the young Lt.

"So how long have you been with the regiment Sir?"

He thought for a moment while he calculated his time in the Army.

"Well I have been in the Army for sixteen months so I guess I would have to say I have been a Para for four months. Oh and you can call me Jack."

"So how come your with us, if you don't mind me asking?"

The Lt looked puzzled, "What do you mean?"

"Come on Sir, people just don't waltz in off Civvy Street straight into Recce Platoon. You're either shit hot and they want to test you to the max or....." he paused, thinking that he may be over stepping the mark with the new officer.

"Or what Mr King? I must be brown nosing someone high up the chain?" he said laughing. "Don't worry Kenny I'm not offended, I understand your concern and I'm sure it will be shared by the other guys too. Especially 2 section when I take over looking after them. Tracey needs a hand out here so I was given the opportunity and wasn't about to turn the chance down to go operational straight away."

"Sorry Sir, I didn't mean to be disrespectful but I appreciate you acknowledging the troops concerns. I didn't know Tracey needed any additional help, he's got us guys after all."

"Like I said Kenny, I'm not offended. I fully understand, I may be the new guy but I ain't stupid," he smiled before continuing. "So how long you been with the regiment and how did you come across Recce?"

"I've been in the Army almost seven years. I've been a Para the whole time and been with Recce for the last four years. I can fill you in on some of your troops if you like? Specialist quals and stuff like that."

"Yeah that would be good."

The young Lt sat back listening to Kenny as he described the skill set of each of the men in his section and the men he would be leading from 2 section before coming to himself.

"Then there's me Sir, I'm a sniper; I've done advanced small arms training, PADI diving training, signals 2 course and I can speak German Sir."

When he'd finished he realised that the Lt had been taking a few notes on the back of a bar napkin.

"That's great Kenny; I really appreciate your help. So I don't have a sniper in my section? How come?" he asked.

"You did have but he bought it a few weeks back on an Op. Private Steve Brice was KIA and to add to that I'm sure you've heard about Sgt Blades?

"Yes, it's a shame about that but Tracey made the right choice in my opinion."

"Fucking right he did Sir, the men are so relieved, especially the guys in 2 section. They didn't know if he was going to kill one of his own if he lost it in the field again. Tracey is a top bloke and I'm not just saying that Jack. I'd follow him into hell's teeth and back again." Kenny spoke passionately as he agreed with his Lt's decision regarding the Sgt.

"So when are you getting your replacements Sir?"

"Good question, we haven't made our decision yet. Tracey and I are going over some files later this evening so he can help me make my decision. So when are you thinking about becoming a Sgt?"

"That's a good question too Sir. I think I'm ready now but I don't want to miss out on the action, plus I either want to go for Pathfinder Platoon or the Regiment." referring to the Elite unit within 5 Airborne Brigade and the SAS.

"I know I'm hardly in a position to give you career advice but if you think you're ready for your Sgt course then I would suggest you go for that and get your money up first then choose your selection. But if you're ready for Pathfinder then why not go straight for 22 Reg?"

"I don't know Sir; my head is a little confused at the moment. I feel like I've come to a crossroads in my career, in my life actually and don't know which road to take."

He sat back drinking another pint of lager brought to him by Black.

The week went by quickly and the tanned men of 1 and 3 sections flew back to Africa. While in the airport the order came to change flights. Lt Briar gathered the men and explained the changes.

"Right gents, there has been a slight change of plan. We're not going back to Niger; we're heading into Chad instead and meeting SFC Heskinski and his merry men to carry out a joint

68

Op. Welcome aboard Lt Mellor, you're about to get your first experience at playing war. Lt Colonel Simpson has sent the order that you're to take 3 section on this one and I'll take 1 section. You've got one hell of team there so you should have no problems."

The seventeen men climbed aboard the military aeroplane and sat in the less than comfortable seating provided, with their kit between their legs for the whole journey. They knew the holiday and R&R was well and truly over. The plane landed in Abeche airport in Chad at 2300 hours and the men of Recce Platoon were met by Sgt John Goldberg (Goldie) of the United States Army Special Forces, the Green Berets. He was SFC Hesk's second in command (2IC).

He introduced himself to the team and they loaded the men onto an old military bus which had seen better days; it was badly banged up with bullet holes along the full length of its body. It had riot meshing against the windows making it difficult to see out which bothered Kenny as he always liked to know where he was going. Sgt Goldie addressed the men from the front of the bus.

"Gentlemen I want to thank you for your support on this joint operation. Capt Silvers generously offered your assistance in taking out a particularly ruthless group of General Gooder's militia. They have set up a training camp here in Chad and we plan to hit it at first light 0500 hours. We should be arriving at the forward attack base at around 0300 hours which will give you time to prep your gear and get ready for war. Although my rank is only equivalent to your Cpl's I will be leading a team of men as equal to your Sgt's. Any questions?"

The two officers threw some quick fire questions which he answered with ease; he obviously knew what he was doing and what he was talking about. After all he was US Special Forces (US SF) and had been for the last five years of his ten year service; previous to that he had served with 82nd Airborne Division.

Kenny advised his men to get their heads down and get as much sleep as they could, it was going to be a long night. He drifted as the bus jolted and rocked its way across country to the forward attack base, which housed thirty members of US Special Forces and the ten deserters from Gooder's militia, who were now working for Hesk. His eyes felt heavy and he finally drifted off to sleep.

Chapter 4

The young Lt Mellor looked at his watch while waiting for the assault to begin; he was down on one knee behind a large stone wall. His thoughts were erratic and he trembled with the anticipation of his first conflict.

"This is it," he said to himself.

Kenny and Sgt Davies were close behind him and noticed his trembling hands.

"Boss," Kenny said with a whisper, "You'll be just fine, it's just like an exercise only they can blow your balls off," he said with a big smile.

The Lt smiled back and relaxed slightly, however his thoughts wouldn't stop spinning around his mind and beads of sweat ran down his back, giving him a chill. It was 0258 hours when he saw out of the corner of his left eye someone signalling him with a red flash light. It was time.

He shuddered and felt like crying, so he blinked excessively to hold back the tears. He heard a noise, PLOP, and seconds later the main gates of the compound disintegrated and chaos broke loose from within the building complex, as enemy soldiers scampered about trying to find their weapons and boots. The US SF soldiers went in first as it was their baby and they wanted to take full credit for the operation and its success.

Lt Mellor and the rest of 3 section sat back

and watched the battle unfold anxiously. They wanted to get into the action despite the fear of what could happen. Death waited around every corner in a fire fight and it wasn't always the best soldiers who survived... usually the luckiest.

Suddenly the rear of the complex erupted with a huge explosion followed by the distinct sound of British issue SA80 rifles and the Minimi LMG. They could hear shouting from within the compound as their friends and the Americans raged war. Kenny's heart was pounding and the young Lt could see it was getting too much for him.

"Hold your position Cpl, and remember why we're here."

"What hiding behind a fucking wall?" he snapped.

Just then they heard screams from inside the gateway; it was one of the deserters working with the Americans. He bellowed for help and was dragging himself out of the complex on his right side. As he came into sight they could see he had been badly injured. The left side of his body was missing, including his arm and shoulder area. Sgt Davies was also getting anxious and was wondering if the teams inside were in trouble.

"Sir I think we better send two men around the back to see what the hell is happening," said the Sgt in a firm but calm tone.

"Sgt Davies I was given strict orders to wait here until we see either the Americans come out successful or we see the green flare go off which will mean it's a GO!"

The Lt was clearly nervous and really didn't want to go running into a death trap if everyone else in there was being slaughtered. Screams came from the centre of the compound. They were English.

The man was screaming, "I'm hit, I'm hit, I can't find my fucking legs."

His cries echoed around the buildings amongst the noise and chaos of the battle.

"That's it, fuck it Sir, sorry but fuck it, I'm going in." Shouted Kenny, and he jumped to his feet and ran towards the entrance.

He scurried close to the wall and as the injured deserter saw Kenny he started to point and scream for help. Kenny raised his rifle, took aim and squeezed the trigger, shooting the man in the face. Lt Mellow looked on in horror at what he had just witnessed.

"Calm down Sir, the guy was already dead. King just put him out of his misery while protecting his and our location. It had to be done," the Sgt said calmly.

Kenny dropped to the ground and crawled to the entrance to take a look. The fighting was still raging and the noise was deafening. He could see five or six US SF soldiers fighting it out with a superior enemy of around twenty men with good defences. He noticed two other men hiding behind a well in the centre of the court yard. It was the deserters; they were cowering in the safety of the well and clearly had no intention of fighting.

Kenny brought his sniper rifle from behind him and got it out of the drag bag. He wasn't a great aim with his left eye but he figured if he could take the leader out then they stood a chance of getting out of there alive. He set his rifle up quickly, adjusting the distance and height on his sight before controlling his breathing and then took aim and fired a single round. The crack and thud were barely heard amongst the other sounds as the gunner fell to the ground. It took Kenny around three seconds to reload, take aim and take out the gunner's number two.

The Americans noticed the drop in fire power and turned to see Kenny at the corner of the wall. POP! went the two UGL's from under the US soldiers M16's causing enough of a distraction for Kenny to take out the officer in charge. He then got up and ran to the well, picking up two enemy AK47's as he went and throwing them at the two deserters.

"Get up and fight or I'll do you myself," said Kenny, firmly yet emotionless.

"Yes Sir," they responded in unison and the youngest man, probably around nineteen years old, stood up and started to fire the weapon.

Kenny moved around the well and took down two more; this gave the Americans the window they needed to move forward. Kenny turned to signal for the two men to follow him when the young man was hit by several rounds to the chest, tumbling backwards. The other man followed Kenny and they made a run for it to the nearest building to the right. Enemy soldiers seemed to be coming out of the woodwork and the assault team would surely be running low on ammo. He could still hear the British man screaming from behind the main building and constant fire from British weapons. Kenny made it to a low wall and saw the source of the enemy replacements, a cellar door with concrete steps going down into darkness. Men crawled from the exit onto the floor and stood up to fight for their leader, General Gooder.

Kenny took his two grenades and pulled the pins, throwing them into the cellar one after another and buried his head in the dirt behind the wall. The explosion shook the ground, his ears rang and his head ached; he turned to grab the other deserter only to find a hole were his face used to be.

"Fuck!" he said out loud. "I got to get through this place."

He heard a shout from his old friend Pte Richard Black.

"Heads down!"

He let loose with the GPMG with a bag magazine of 500 rounds in it, slung around his neck. It was like a scene from Rambo and Kenny couldn't believe his luck, he hit the ground yet again keeping one eye on the opening from which the enemy were coming. They were *still* pushing forward and obviously assumed the attackers had got lucky.

Black didn't come any further into the compound, he stood at the entrance letting round after round pound the face of the building and destroying anything that stood up. Sgt Davies landed next to Kenny and patted him on the helmet.

"Hey up Kenny boy, thought you might need a hand over here," he said laughing.

Davies saw the same thing Kenny was looking at and grabbed a belt of ten grenades from around his head and pulled two, throwing them together at the exit before hitting the deck. Only this time as soon as the explosion went off they both jumped to their feet. Knowing each other's thoughts and moves they ran to the door and opened up with their rifles; Kenny with the LSW and the Sgt with his Colt Commando, a short robust version of the M16. They emptied a full magazine, before dropping another two grenades into the hole and jumping to the side out of harm's way.

Suddenly the whole building shook. They both fell to the floor wondering what the hell had just happened. Davies looked up to see the building collapsing down on him; he jumped to his feet and made a run for it. The large chunks of rubble missed him by a whisker but a lot of debris caught his back and legs, causing dozens of cuts and grazes. He turned back to see where Kenny was, but he was out of sight. He shouted after him but got no response.

Machine gun fire opened up to the front of the complex and yard area from the secondary buildings behind. He ran as a zig zag across the yard trying to avoid being hit. Black was firing from the hip as he popped around the corner every few seconds trying to give covering fire.

Sgt Davies made it around the corner of the entrance gate wall to find most of 3 section hiding in its cover.

"We're running low on ammo and I don't think we're going to make a damn bit of difference now Sgt. I suggest we retreat and get the fuck out of dodge," the Lt said in a panicked voice.

"But boss, we've got men in there. We don't just abandon our own or even those stupid yank bastards who got us in this shit in the first place and where the fuck is Stone and Cassum?"

"They've gone to see what's going on around the back just like you and King said they should."

"Well how long they been gone?" He asked as he felt a sinking feeling in the pit of his stomach.

"I don't know, maybe ten minutes. They should be back any time now; I gave them strict orders not to engage the enemy but to report back with a SITREP."

The remaining men of 3 section had no

choice but to withdraw. Sgt Davies led them back to relative safety in a wooded area roughly 1km away from the compound and 800 metres from the ERV. They sat down for a moment catching their breath and the Sgt looked around at who was left in his team. There was himself, the Lt, Black, McMann and Moore, five men of an eight man team and he was pretty sure Kenny and the others were dead. He had to fight back the tears of his loss and focus on getting his men to safety and the ERV or they would all be dead within the hour.

He got up and gathered the men before running off at speed, as they approached the ERV he could see movement in the dry yellow grass and some low rocks near the pick up point.

"Fuck, we need to know if it's friendly or not and there's only one fucking way to do that," said the Sgt clearly reaching breaking point. He crawled closer to the position and said the password quietly, "Bangkok!"

The relieved response came back, "Pussy." Stone lifted his head up to see the Sgt's face and gave a relieved grin before continuing. "They're fucking dead Bri, loads of them. I couldn't do anything about it mate, it was crazy."

"Don't worry about that, I'm just glad to see you in one piece ya crazy Manc."

They radioed for the pick up and were instructed to move a further 3km away from the compound for safety reasons, the chopper simply didn't want to get shot down and there was a high likelihood if they went into the kill zone. As they boarded the Sea King helicopter there was sigh of relief as well as a sigh of sadness. Davies looked over at Pte Black and saw a shadow of a man with dead eyes mourning the loss of his best friend.

They were taken to an American base in Chad which housed the 82nd Airborne and US SF units; they touched down and were immediately taken into the hospital tent to be checked over. Davies was sitting next to the Lt discussing what they would report back as the second chopper returned. A small American heli, the HH-65A Dolphin, came in hard and fast with emergency casualties from the same battle. They ran over to see what was going on and were horrified when they saw the condition of some of the men being carried out; they saw three US uniforms and one African from a deserter. Then out popped the men of 1 section; Sgt Fisher, Lt Briar, Cpl Taylor and Pte Frost all seemed to be uninjured other than a few knocks and bumps. Out on a stretcher came a real sight for sore eyes. Cpl Kenny King was lying there, bloody clothing covering most of his body. Davies shouted back to the tent, "Black, Heads up we've got a visitor for you."

Black came running out of the tent with the drip still in his arm, he was seriously dehydrated but ran to see his friend. As he got to him he looked down to see an injured man but couldn't see his injuries.

"Kenny, where the fuck you hit man?" he asked desperately.

He groaned as he tried to explain, "I don't know if I *am* hit. I had the empire state building come down on me you nob head," as he gave a forced smile to his friend.

"Fuck me man, you really are indestructible ya tough Yorkshire bastard," he was so pleased to see Kenny he burst into tears as they rushed him off to be checked out.

Sgt Davies and the Lt walked over to him and put a hand on each shoulder. There were no words, they too were glad to see King back in one piece.

Out of the thirty US SF troops only four survived. None of the deserters lived and 3 section lost Pte John Cassum, he was 20 years old and a good soldier. He died trying to give covering fire for 1 section that was pinned down with little chance of getting out alive; he gave his life for his friends and colleagues. He was later awarded the Military Cross posthumously for his gallantry and valour, Kenny was also awarded the Military Cross.

The operation had been a complete failure with many lives lost and the General and his henchmen continued to reign over the region. The Para's returned to their camp in Niger and was greeted by old friends who had heard the news and to pass condolences. Two weeks later the men of 2 Para returned to the UK heroes, where they would stay for the next four months until their next tour of Northern Ireland (NI).

Chapter 5

The men of 2 Para had been back four weeks and Kenny was on his feet training as if the injuries had never occurred. Luckily he suffered minor injuries under the collapse of the building. Three broken ribs and a fracture in his right forearm.

He joined the men of Recce Platoon on their daily eight mile run, as they pounded the streets of Colchester. This was to be the new base for 2 Para who were moving from Aldershot over the next six months. The CO decided it would be good for the Recce Platoon to get settled in, in case the move happened while they were on tour in Northern Ireland. 2 Para have spent more time in NI than any other infantry regiment in the British Army. They have permanent bases in South Armagh and Belfast from which they launch their patrols and operations from; surprisingly the base has only come under mortar attack twice in all its years there.

As Kenny ran at the front of the group of twenty men he breathed calmly and easily, his mind flashed back to the days when he didn't believe he would amount to anything. A chubby kid who could sprint and had the weight to be a good rugby player but when he thought of joining the Army he really didn't know what he wanted to be other than an infantry soldier. He remembered the day he walked into the Army Careers Office in Leeds City centre; it had all these colourful pictures of soldiers taking part in military exercises and outdoor pursuits. It looked very enticing.

He arrived at the door and rang the bell. He stood there for a couple of minutes watching the two soldiers chatting and deliberately taking their time to get up and answer. He rang it again wondering if they had heard him; a large man stood up and put on his maroon beret. He was a Paratrooper and was wearing the green flashes on his arm of 3 Para. He must have been 5ft 10 and was built like a brick shithouse. He opened the door, annoyed that he had been disturbed.

"Yeah, what do you want?" he snarled.

"I want to enquire about joining the Army," Kenny responded meekly.

"Oh you do, do ya? Well get your arse in off the street. We don't want people seeing a tart like you littering the neighbourhood now do we?" he said with an evil grin.

"Give the boy a break Bill," said the older gentleman sitting behind the desk. "Come and have a seat son, my name is Staff Sgt Brooks and this charming fella is Cpl Stevens of 3 Para."

"Yes, I saw the flashes on his arm. I'm interested in joining the Infantry and thought about the Para's."

"Oh you did, did ya?" questioned Cpl Stevens. "So you think you're hard enough to join my Regiment?"

"I don't know if I'm hard or not. I just think I have something to offer and I've heard you have to be really determined to pass the Para's."

"Ok lad, let's start by taking some details down and then we'll show you what's available to you depending on your score in the written test. How old are you in years and months?" the Staff Sgt asked.

"I'm seventeen and one month," he replied.

"Ok son, then by the time you got in you'd be classed as a young soldier coz you're too old to be a junior and too young to be classed as an adult, but you'd go through the same training as an adult soldier. Do you understand?"

"Yes," Kenny responded, feeling fear taking hold of him, or was it excitement?

Kenny suddenly felt very alive at the prospect at being called a young soldier, as if the air felt cleaner somehow. After he had watched a video all about the different sectors within the British Army the Staff Sgt and Cpl continued to discuss everything about the Army and gave him an information pack to take home. When it got to the part about the infantry he got particularly excited, especially when he saw men throwing themselves out of the back of a Hercules.

He left the office that day with a date for the following week to come back and take the test and have a medical examination in the back office with a nurse. He was so excited that as soon as he got home he put on his training clothes and went out for a run. Up until this stage Kenny had only been able to manage running three miles without stopping other than playing Rugby which involved lots of sprinting. As soon as he crossed that distance he ran out of steam and had to stop for a rest and then ended up walking the rest of the way home feeling like a failure.

Now he had new purpose, plus he had seen the kind of distances that would be expected of him in training, so he set off on a route that he knew to be exactly five miles long. As Kenny reached the part he knew to be the three mile mark he could feel himself slowing down again. He thought back to the Para Cpl in the recruitment office who was about an inch taller than himself and of similar build, only more solid and muscular. With that in mind he got a burst of energy and increased his speed again, continuing for the remainder of the run without stopping. This achievement made him feel great, plus he had conquered a new barrier in his mind. He felt that he could achieve anything now.

He passed his written test and medical with ease and Staff Sgt Brooks gave him his options and advised him that he shouldn't believe all the hype about the Para's as there were plenty of good infantry regiments in the Army, or indeed other none infantry regiments to choose from.

"Ok son, this is how it is. At the moment you can apply to join the following units; Royal Engineers,

Royal Corps of Transport, Royal Artillery, any infantry regiment including the Parachute Regiment and the Medical Corps. So what do you think takes your fancy? You have to choose three in case you don't get a place in the first choice, most people do get their first choice but it's standard procedure."

Brooks sat back and watched the young boy as he pondered his future. He already knew what Kenny was about to say, he only wanted to become an infantry soldier and he wanted to be the best.

"Ok I've made my choices. I'd like to apply for the Parachute Regiment as my first choice, the Royal Green Jackets and finally the Coldstream Guards if that's ok Staff?"

"You do realise that you've picked the three toughest infantry units in the British Army don't you?" questioned the Staff Sgt, "It's not going to be easy no matter which unit you get in."

"I know but it's what I really want to do. If I'm going to be a soldier I want to be the best."

"Ok son. The next stage is to send you to Sutton Coldfield where you'll undergo the Army selection course. The only thing that will be different from the rest of the guys there is you will have to do more than everyone else in order to impress. Plus you have to do tricep dips on parallel bars and then on the run when everyone else stops after one mile you will have to do two miles in less than seventeen and a half minutes. Do you think you

86

can do that?"

"I think so, I'm a Rugby player so I'm more of a sprinter than a runner but I'll train harder to make sure I'm ready for it all, and the other tests don't sound too bad."

"Good then get your backside into shape and I'd recommend you drop at least a stone before you get there and probably another stone by the time you get to Aldershot, providing you're successful of course," he said with a smile of encouragement.

He liked Staff Sgt Brooks and hoped there would be more soldiers like him in the Army to offer encouragement as they went through the toughest training in the world. Kenny increased his training, constantly testing himself and joined a gym where he took advice on how to drop weight quickly.

His training schedule was relentless. Day one would include a mile long swim in the morning and a five mine run in the evening. Day two involved an hour of weights before breakfast and hill sprints for thirty minutes before bed. Day three, Kenny had to add a mile to his run before his usual rugby training and circuits for two hours in the afternoon. Another mile swim and weights were in line for day four, and day five's six mile run and further circuit training seemed daunting. Thankfully, he'd allowed a rest day before a morning rugby match and weight training on the final, seventh day.

When Kenny arrived at Sutton Coldfield he felt ready. There had been a two month wait for his selection course since he was last in the Army careers office in Leeds and he knew he wouldn't be allowed to join before he was seventeen and a half years old. They were welcomed to the base and told the rules and regulations they had to follow, then given their room numbers to split them up away from any possible friends. This was part of the plan to make them branch out and meet new people as much as anything else. Kenny was in a room with three others. There was a black guy, Harry Webb from Birmingham. Kenny had never met a black person to talk to before and found it a little strange, and a completely different experience, which he quite liked. The other two guys were Matthew Hand from London and Steve McGregor from Glasgow. Harry was probably the most confident, being a little older than the rest, so he started up the conversation.

"How old are you guys and what regiments you all joining?" Harry asked.

"I'm seventeen and joining the Para's," responded Kenny.

"Eighteen and the Para's," said Matthew rather sheepishly.

"Twenty and I'm gonna guess we're all joining the Para's," said Steve in a gruff Scottish accent.

They all laughed before Harry responded and surprised the group with his age.

"I'm twenty five and yes I too am going to be a

Para."

"Wow! Twenty five, you don't look any older than Steve," Kenny said, flabbergasted at how young Harry looked

"Thanks a fucking bunch," said Steve, "does that mean I look like this old bastard?"

The room burst into laughter and the young men sat chatting for the next hour while waiting for dinner call. They sat together and all had a common goal. They were all here to become paratroopers. This set them apart from the rest immediately; they knew they had to be fitter and stronger than the rest of the recruits here to join other regiments.

The next day after breakfast they had a series of lectures and talks about the Army and the fitness tests they were about to undertake. They were taken to a dark room which felt like a warehouse with wooden boxes fixed to the floor, this was the first test. They had to step up and down in time with the recorded timer for a total of ten minutes and then take their pulse rates for one minute and give them to the instructors who were recording all of the results. They then went over to the gym. It was just like a school gymnasium with wooden beams that could be pulled out and set to different heights, and there was a chart on a wall that they had to jump and reach, sixteen inches above their own height with their hand stretched upwards.

Kenny was at the jump first and hit the marker with his wet finger tips at eighteen inches, first pass. Then he went on to the beam to do his under grasp pull ups; he achieved the maximum score of thirteen pull ups before moving onto the incline sit up bench where he had to do twenty. Again he passed and moved onto the parallel bars and completed his thirteen tricep dips with ease. Some guys couldn't do one without shaking uncontrollably and falling off, so the PTI called everyone who was applying for the Parachute Regiment over to the bars, there was ten in total.

"Right lads, listen up. I can't fucking believe just how many of you have never done this exercise before. It's not that hard. I'm going to get young Mr King up here now to show you how it's done and I don't want him to stop until his arms fall off."

Kenny wasn't sure if the instructor was joking so he got into position and started knocking out tricep dips in a slow and steady fashion. One after another he ploughed through the exercise like his arms were a piece of machinery, separate from the rest of his body. When he got to thirty reps his arms began to shake and he gave up at thirty five speaking to the PTI with disappointment on his face.

"I'm sorry Cpl that's all I can do."

Laughter exploded from all the instructors in the room and so the recruits joined in. Some of the kids on selection couldn't believe it. They had never seen anyone do so many dips before. As they moved outside to the running track Harry whispered to Kenny.

"Nice one mate, you're a fucking Para in the making, you're an animal."

They grinned at each other as they walked to the start line. They followed the Cpl leading the run, as he ran the first mile at a pace of exactly ten minutes before shouting go, as the other regiments in the Army started their one mile run, to be completed in under eight and a half minutes. The potential Para's did their two miles in less than seventeen and a half minutes. Out of the Para recruits Harry was the first to come in by a long way. At the end of the run the PTI stood the men together as he shouted out their results.

Webb made it in 12 minutes 3 seconds, and King in 13 minutes flat. Hampshire, 14 minutes flat and Hand 14 minutes 21 seconds. Anderson took 14 minutes 53 and Brass 15 minute flat, whilst McGregor and Pendlington took 15 minutes 50 seconds and Binns 17. Finally, Wolrich finished in 17 minutes 30 seconds exactly.

"You're in by the skin of your teeth sunshine." Shouted the instructor.

They celebrated in the NAAFI later that evening with the one pint of beer they were allowed, and slept like babies before getting up the next day and returning home. Before they left they had an interview with the CO of recruit selection and the

Para selectees were the first to be seen by the officer in charge. They were called in alphabetical order so they waited, standing to attention in the corridor outside the CO's office.

"King," shouted the Lt Colonel.

Kenny marched into his office and stood to attention before him, the officer didn't look up from his paperwork as he spoke.

"Be seated," he said. "How do you think you did in the tests?"

"I think I did ok Sir," said Kenny feeling very nervous.

"Do you indeed? I've seen better but as you said, you did ok. However, ok isn't enough for the Parachute Regiment young man and I'm curious as to whether you have what it takes to push beyond your limits."

Kenny stood there silently unsure of what to say next.

"I think I can do better by the time I get there Sir."

"Good answer King, good answer. Your damn right too, you're going to have to shed a bit of that puppy fat you're carrying too."

"Yes Sir, I have shed seventeen pounds prior to coming here so I'm confident I can drop another stone at least."

"So how far are you running currently?"

"I do eighteen miles per week in three runs, plus I play Rugby so do a lot of sprint training Sir," Kenny responded feeling confident.

"It's not enough!" the Lt Colonel snapped sharply.

"You need to be running at least six miles per day and you should start carrying weight on your back, at least twenty five pounds and work your way up to forty two pounds. Do you understand? Do you think you can do that?"

"I'll get right on it Sir. Can I ask Sir what kind of back pack I'll need as I don't have a lot of money and have never bought one before?"

The officer was pleased with his responses and questions; it showed the young man in front of him was serious about his career choice. There was no hesitation, he was sure of his answers. The Lt Colonel discussed and advised King before asking him to leave and congratulating him as he walked out of the door. Kenny walked out of there feeling like a giant peacock with his feathers spanning out wide across the corridor, he felt like he was already a Paratrooper.

He returned home and began his training immediately, his schedule was increased and he took the advice from the officer deadly serious. He bought a book on the Parachute Regiment and started reading about its history, learning as much as he could in preparation. Three weeks later he got the letter instructing him that he was invited to Browning Barracks Depot Para in Aldershot and he had eight weeks to prepare.

His training didn't waiver for anything, his whole life revolved around it. He had no time for girlfriends and he had already given up spending time with most of his friends from school and Rugby. He felt he was ready to live up to The Parachute Regiments motto, 'Utrinque Paratus' ('Ready for Anything').

Chapter 6

As the run with the Recce Platoon came to an end, Kenny returned from his day dream, reminiscing about the past with a smile. After he showered and got into his uniform he was called for a Junior NCO's meeting in the NAAFI bar. He could smell the coffee and bacon sandwiches as he got to the top of the staircase.

He entered the room to see some of the guys he had served with and a couple of new faces, they were either newly promoted Cpls, or new to Recce Platoon. At the front stood Lt Briar and the Regimental Sergeant Major (RSM), Warrant Officer first class (WO1) Mark Foley, Lt Briar took a register.

In 1 section there was Cpl Taylor, Harrison and Lance Cpl Bell. In 2, there was Cpl Stevens and Bands. 3 section included Cpl Moore and King, and those new faces were named Cpl Stafford, Malarkey and Lance Cpl Bond.

The three new Cpls were introduced to the rest of the team as being new to Recce Platoon. They had come from different companies within 2 para and had their own skill set which would hopefully replace the losses Recce had suffered in Africa. Lt Briar began the meeting.

"Gentlemen we have a lot of work to do before we head to NI and only eight weeks to do it. I want the men in tip top condition, especially those currently nursing injuries. We're going in with the rest of C Coy and there are high expectations on us. Not that there isn't normally but they're expecting some heavy shit to kick off in the next three to six months and it looks like we'll be in the thick of it for a change." He paused and scanned the room watching as the Junior NCO's scribbled in note pads. "Any questions so far?" he asked.

Kenny was the first to speak up, "Boss, are the sections staying the same or is there going to be a shake up? I only ask because of the casualties we took and the new guys on board."

"Quite right King, there will be some slight changes which I will come to shortly. For the benefit of Stafford, Malarkey and Bond I think I should explain. We lost three men on the last Op in Africa, two dead and one is in prison."

"Yes, we heard about Sgt Blades Sir," said Malarkey saving the Lt the time it would take to explain the whole thing.

"Ok then let's carry on with the detail."

Lt Briar went through the location of their base in Ireland and after 90 minutes of discussion decided it was time to inform them of the new section layout.

"Right men, some of you might not like the new layout but that's just how it is so there's no use getting upset about it. I have already briefed Sgt's Davies, Fisher and," the Lt stopped dead in his tracks realising he had almost let the cat out of the bag, "let's give you the section layout shall we."

"Boss, you didn't mention who the third Sgt is," said Cpl Moore of 2 section.

"As I was saying," he responded curtly.

"Shut your fucking cake hole," snarled RSM Foley.

"Yes Sir," responded Moore, smirking at Kenny who was to his left.

The Lt called out the rota for 1 section first followed by 3 section. Kenny noticed he had been kicked out of his own section and wasn't happy about it at all. Moore looked at Kenny with a smile as if he could see what was coming but Kenny didn't see the next rota coming at all.

In 1st section there would be Sgt Bill Fisher, Cpls Steve Taylor, Michael Malarkey and Phil Harrison, with Privates David Frost, Tony Bowers, Colin Stenner and finally Carl Dunn. In 2 section is Acting Sgt Kenny King, accompanying Cpls Andrew Stafford, Phil Stevens and Daniel Bands, alongside Lance Cpl David Bond and Privates Robert Newland, Jason Sanders and Matthew Hand. Then finally, 3 section included Sgt Brian Davies, Cpl Jack Rust, Lance Cpl Fred Bell and Privates David Brown, Thomas Harris, Richard Black, Sandy McMann and Phil Price. There were three medics assigned, Private Arthur Wilson for 1 section, Lance Cpl Edgar Stollers for 2 section and for the 3rd, Lance Cpl Iain Chaplin.

"So acting Sgt King I would like to congratulate you on your trial promotion. You are only going to NI for the next three months then you'll be coming home to attend the Senior Command Course to attain your official Sgt's rank. Congratulations Kenny."

The room erupted with applause for Kenny and the RSM walked over and placed his hand on his back before speaking.

"Well King, I can't think of anyone better to lead those men. You're a solid combat leader with a bright future ahead of you with the regiment. You won't get a pay rise until you actually hold the official rank but its all good experience for you."

"Yes Sir, I know. It just took me by surprise that's all; I really didn't see *that* coming. It's a shame about losing my section though I have to admit, I'm gonna miss that fucker Black." Kenny knew only too well that Black would be devastated at losing him to another section, even though he knew there was no-one who deserved it more than him. The meeting was closed so the NCO's walked over to the office block and up to the third floor lecture room, where the remaining men from Recce Platoon awaited what they thought was the NI briefing, which it was but with the latest twist of the restructure of the three sections. As the NCO's entered the room Sgt Davies and Fisher stood at the front next to the black board. There were a few grumbles and banter thrown around until everyone sat down ready for the brief.

The team brief was usually carried out by the Sgts but when Kenny didn't sit down with the men his old friend Black decided it was time for some more abuse.

"Hey Kenny are you lost, sit your fat arse down here next to me or people will think you're in charge or something," he laughed.

Kenny addressed the room, "Okay gents, there has been a restructure of the sections and they are as follows." He read out the names of each section and left 2 section till last. "The men of two section are in for a real treat coz you got me as your section commander, for those of you who don't know me my name is Acting Sgt Kenny King."

The room was stunned at the changes; Black just sat there staring at his friend.

"Wait up a minute Kenny, what the fuck is going on? You can't leave me behind."

"Sorry mate, shit happens. Anyway you should be glad, your life is about to get a whole lot easier without me to look after," he said jokingly.

"Fuck me mate, I mean congratulations and all that but I'm fucking gutted to be losing you. You're the best Cpl in the Para's and well I'm gonna fucking miss ya you fat twat."

It was obvious that Black was upset despite his bantering and Sgt Davies knew he'd have to keep an eye on him to make sure he didn't let it get him down.

Sgt King spoke to the room again, "Right men we've got a lot to do in preparation for NI but in the mean time we'll be training like fuck to get into the best shape you've ever been in. Now there are six new faces in the Platoon so let's make them welcome. Cpl Stafford, what was the daily run like in C Coy?"

"It was the usual eight mile run in PT rig," he responded.

"PT rig, you're kidding me right?" Kenny quizzed.

"No Sgt that's standard procedure for all companies now. No boots or webbing to reduce injuries."

"Well lads you can kiss that little jolly goodbye, we usually do three different runs per week. We start the week with the standard 8 mile run in boots, no gear. Then we do a 10 miler in full combat webbing and clothing, only 32lbs though and finally we do a 13 miler in full combat gear weighing 42 lbs. I hope you all enjoy training coz in Recce Platoon we fucking live for it!"

He was grinning like a Cheshire cat with excitement. They ran through the NI briefing and then broke for lunch.

"I want you all fell in outside the gym at 1400hors in your running gear, that's boots, lightweights and a t-shirt for the new boys," Kenny shouted with enthusiasm.

He went off and got ready with the other Sgts. Sgt Davies sat next to him on the bench while he checked his webbing for rattles.

"This lot are gonna fucking love you Kenny," Davies said sarcastically.

"Why's that then?" Kenny responded.

"The guys fresh in from Company are not used to working at this level, its gonna be a real eye opener for them, plus I know your thinking of upping the game a little so your boys are the toughest bastards in the Platoon."

"Nothing wrong with that, is there mate?" he smiled.

"No mate, there isn't but you got to make sure you don't injure them. The boss was pretty fucking clear that he wants men ready to fight when they hit the ground and he wants any casualties to be binned out of the unit."

"Shit, really? I didn't know he wanted to bin people," Kenny was now thinking he would have to hold back on the training a little, which disappointed him.

"Listen Kenny, we go back a long way and I'm over the fucking moon you've been given this Acting Sgt gig but you got to start thinking like a Sgt too. This isn't a lecture or anything, just some friendly advice. You okay with that mate?"

"Of course I am Bri, like you said we go back a long way. Thanks mate, I appreciate it."

Kenny went back to sorting his gear while the other Sgts did the same before walking over to the Sgt's mess where he was introduced to the staff and given a menu for the week so he could pick what he wanted. He couldn't believe the difference in service; he'd never been asked what he wanted to eat before and was a little taken aback by it all. He ticked the boxes and handed it back to a lady who was originally from the Caribbean. He decided to ask her about her nationality, hoping not to offend her.

"So where about are you from Ma'am if you don't mind me asking?"

"I'm from Trinidad, where are you from Sgt?" she asked smiling at his naivety.

She thought he was very sweet for asking so politely, it was obvious that he wasn't used to speaking to the staff on site and he was very curious. It was almost childlike of him but she liked it and decided to humour him. They chatted for five minutes while he grabbed a chicken and stuffing sandwich from her and then had to excuse himself, as he wanted to be waiting for the men when they arrived. He was standing chatting to the other Sgts and Lt Briar when they gathered and fell in; Lt Briar had decided to join them.

"Afternoon gents, I'll be joining you today. We're going to do a little 8 mile run to evaluate your current fitness levels and from there the Sgts will organise a training regime to fit his own sections strengths and weaknesses. If anyone is nursing an injury make your Sgt aware and let's get you to physio. I don't want any broken bodies joining us in NI when we go in eight weeks time. Eight weeks isn't a lot of time so you'll be worked harder than usual but I want fit men not fucked men, so get your injuries in check or you'll be out of Recce Platoon and back in the companies. Do I make myself clear?"

A resounding "Yes Sir!" rang out as they stood to attention. It was unusual for them to be stood on parade this way, things were normally a little more relaxed and the men could tell something had gone on for such changes to be made. Black decided he would be the one to ask.

"Sir, permission to speak Sir?"

"What is it Private Black?" Briar said, sounding annoyed.

"What's with all the change Sir? I mean, no disrespect to anyone but we don't normally stand to attention to be briefed and there seems to be a lot of changes in the wings Sir."

"Seeing that you've asked, it's because I've had my bollocks ripped off by the newly promoted Major Silvers. He said I've let the standards slip and that we are to remember who we are. We're the top soldiers in an elite fighting unit. We are first and foremost Paratroopers and you lot looked like a bag of shit every time he saw you."

Lt Briar was furious, but it wasn't at Black's question, it was the fact that he actually agreed with the Major.

"Yes Sir, sorry Sir," Black responded realising he had kicked the hornets' nest.

Sgt Fisher took control of the Platoon and led the route. Davies and King were doing the analysing of the men while Sgt Fisher kept the pace. There were one or two who needed to improve their fitness drastically if they wanted to stay with the unit, surprisingly Private Price seemed to be suffering. He was a fit guy who didn't usually struggle. This concerned Kenny as he definitely didn't want to lose Price, plus he also knew that he had aspirations of joining the SAS in the next year or two and it wouldn't bode well if he was kicked out of Recce Platoon for lack of fitness.

At the end of the run each Sgt took their men to a different corner of the gym and put them through some circuits and sprints before finally dismissing them. The Sgts chatted about the areas they needed to work on as a platoon and asked each other about the strengths and weaknesses of each man in their sections.

"I was really surprised to see Price at the back Bri, what the fucks going on with him?" Kenny asked.

"I'm not sure mate. He had a touch of cold the other week that seemed to floor him. I think I'll have the doc check him out in case he caught something dodgy while in Africa but I fucking hope not coz he's one of the best men I've got at that level," he said equally concerned.

"What about Frost and Dunn? They were a sack of shit today," said Kenny to Sgt Fisher.

"Yeah I know, I gave them hell when we got back in. I'm getting fucking sick of mollycoddling these fuckers; they need to grow a pair of big fat hairy bollocks like us."

They all laughed at Fishers comment but they were all worried about some of the regular soldiers who didn't seem to be pulling their weight in training, and they wondered if some of them wanted out of Recce and back to their old units. They decided to confront them on a one on one basis to alleviate the embarrassment, but when they were asked they all said they wanted to continue and most were surprised at being asked. It was the wakeup call they needed.

Several weeks had gone by when the order came to saddle up and get ready to move to NI. The site was a frenzy of activity as the Coldstream Guards were also heading to NI at the same time as 2 Para. Sgt Davies and Fisher were chatting with Lt Briar and Major Silvers when Kenny and the rest of 2 section came into view.

"Well fuck me, here comes guts and glory!" said Sgt Fisher sarcastically.

"That's enough of that Sgt," Lt Briar snapped.

"Sorry Sir," he winced, realising he had crossed the line of professionalism in front of a senior officer.

The men were weighed down under heavy Bergen's and looked exhausted as they came marching past them. King called out the command.

"Officer to your left side, eyes left. Quick march, left, right, left, right," and he carried on past the Lt and Major having saluted them accordingly.

"Sgt King," called Lt Briar, "Once you stand the

men down can you come back and speak to me please?"

"Yes Sir, I'll be two minutes."

The two Sgts went their separate ways to check on their men and to get their own affairs in order. Kenny speed marched back up the slight incline to where the Lt and Major were standing.

"Sir you wanted to see me?"

Major Silvers was the first to respond, "Cpl King, were you not told that these men were to be prepared for their tour of Ireland in tip top condition?"

"Yes Sir," he responded crisply.

"So what the fuck are you doing to my troops?" snapped Silvers.

"Sir your troops are in tip top shape for the tour. I have taken them from the under achieving section that you informed me they were and have turned them back into Recce Troops of the highest standard. There isn't one man Jack in Recce Platoon who will touch my men physically or strategically!"

Kenny was pissed off by the Major's comments and it was noticed by both officers.

"Sgt King," Lt Briar emphasised his rank to the Major, "You had better square that attitude away when speaking to an officer, do you understand me?"

"Yes Sir, perfectly. With all due respect Major Silvers you were the one who told me to shake things up and I have followed that order to the letter. What I have produced is a team of highly skilled and physically fit animals we call paratroopers. I hardly think I should be reprimanded for that Sir."

The two officers stood for a moment waiting for each other to speak; the Major broke the silence.

"So what you're telling me is that 2 section are the dog's bollocks after just eight weeks under your command Sgt King?"

"Yes Sir, that's exactly what I'm saying," he said proudly.

"That is a very bold claim to make," said Lt Briar knowing the standard of King's old section. "You're telling me that you have trained these guys to be better than the unbeatable 3 section? You're original section?"

"There was a reason they were the best Sir," Kenny said cockily and all three of them laughed at his confidence.

"Okay Sgt, the proof will be in the pudding over the next three months in Ireland. Won't it? So what have the men just finished?" asked the Major.

"Yes Sir I guess it will. They've just done a 20 miler carrying 80lbs Sir, all good stuff Sir," he said with a broad smile across his face.

They dismissed him and walked back to the officer's mess to enjoy the comfort of their lounge and a glass of sherry. They sat down in the soft leather chairs near the roaring fire, with a painting of their Commander in Chief, Prince Charles in his

Para uniform above it, standing proud.

"Tracey that fellow of yours is a cocky little sod isn't he? I'm not sure how to take him sometimes. I mean he's a solid combat soldier and a well respected section leader as a Cpl but is he ready for his third stripe?" asked the Major.

"I think so Malcolm, like you said he's a great section leader so why wouldn't he make a great platoon commander? I think he'll be fine once he's done the seniors course, which should give him the tools required to do the job. I would still like to give him the chance to prove himself in NI before we consider taking it off him if that's okay with you?"

"Of course it is, you're the boss Tracey I was simply giving you my views. I don't want you to take it away from him. I'm just a little concerned about his mentality sometimes. It will be interesting to see if his claim is as good as his word. I mean he basically said Sgt Davies isn't responsible for the standards of the section, but he is. Very ballsy claim don't you think?" he asked, raising an eyebrow while taking a sip of his sherry.

"Yeah it's a ballsy statement but in some ways I can't help thinking he's telling the truth. Don't get me wrong Brian is a good platoon leader but he does get a little flustered sometimes when under combat stress situations. He deals with them but Kenny seems to step in and take over from time to time. I think they've worked great together over the last three years."

Major Silvers and Lt Briar sat quietly for a few moments while they both thought about what was being said, the Major sighed before beginning again.

"So are we saying that maybe we need to evaluate Sgt Davies while in NI?"

"I'm starting to wonder about that myself actually. I mean Fisher hasn't got a scratch on either of the other two to be honest but he did rise to the challenge in Africa and did a bloody good job too," Lt Briar paused to think about his next statement carefully.

"Bloody hell Tracey it sounds like the whole senior NCO team are fucked up," they both chuckled at how bad it sounded. "Let's not let that get around or people will think the dogs of war have been tamed."

"Who the hell gave them that name anyway?" the young Lt enquired smiling at the bravado of it all.

Major Silvers couldn't stop laughing and the Lt wondered why it was so funny.

"Sir is there something I should know?" asked the Lt.

"It was me Tracey; well it was kind of me. I was observing 3 section one day out in the field, I think it was Mogadishu but it could have been Ethiopia and yes, I know they're two completely different places before you think I've lost the plot," he smiled and then continued with his story. "I was with Colonel Marshall of the Grenadier Guards and Brigadier Sharp of 5 Airborne Brigade when we saw 3 section pinned down by enemy fire. I was just about to scream at the Captain in charge at the time when the most amazing display of gallantry unfolded before us. A private whose name I didn't know at the time stood up and just went for the machine gun post that was pinning them down. Then we noticed a second private doing the same damn thing. They worked together like clockwork; it was amazing to see, especially as they took out the machine gun and continued forward to annihilate the enemy forces."

The Major was grinning from ear to ear as he paused for thought.

"The Brigadier asked who the hell are those men and I replied, "they are the dogs of war Sir" and the old bugger was so proud of them he told me to give them a medal each. I later found out it was none other than Private Kenny King and Private Richard Black, so I awarded them both the Queens Gallantry Medal (QGM)."

"So that's how they got that medal, Jesus H Christ Malcolm I never knew that and I've been in charge of them for the last twelve months. I can't believe that's how they got the name," Lt Briar was shocked and pleased at the same time. "You know King has also been awarded the Military Cross (MC)?"

"Yes I know, he's one of the most highly decorated Cpl in 2 Para! Of course I know! What do you think I am, some kind of moron?"

The Major seemed annoyed at the Lt's

comment but shrugged it off with a smile. They chatted a little while longer before retiring to their own quarters. The Lt had to get his own kit ready but the Major would have his done for him so didn't need to worry about the little things, like packing.

Chapter 7

They arrived at the barracks in County Antrim at 0500 on the Saturday morning after a rough flight over from England. The weather had been atrocious and a Hercules isn't renowned for its comfort for passengers.

The men got settled into their rooms while the three Sgts went off to meet the other senior NCO's from 2 Para's A, B and C Coy's. The Sgt's mess wasn't anything special, a simple lounge area big enough for around twenty men with a big old colour cigarette stained TV in the corner and a games room with a six foot pool table with torn cloth. The facilities were basic but clean and it was adequate for what they needed, after all they had experienced much worse living conditions in other countries.

It was a particularly grey day, the kind that could easily have depressed a man if they let it. The men introduced each other to people who they hadn't met before and a couple of the Sgts from 2 Para congratulated Kenny on his promotion. Kenny thought he better put them straight before the rumours got out about it being an acting role for three months.

"Kenny my man, well done on the promotion mate, you deserve it! It's been a long time coming though ain't it?" said Sgt Hall of C Coy.

"Well it's only an acting position for now until I do my seniors course in three months time," said Kenny.

"Oh don't worry about that, you'll breeze the course. I've known you a long time and I know there's one thing you're good at and that's delivering the goods when needed."

Sgt Davies piped up adding to the conversation.

"Did he tell you what Captain Silvers, oops sorry Major Silvers said to him a few weeks back?"

"No what was that then?" Hall asked curiously.

"He was telling Kenny that he would congratulate him if he passed the course and warned him that he shouldn't be too confident as it was really tough and lots of people underestimate it."

Davies laughed as he told the story.

"So why was that so funny?" asked another Sgt from A Coy.

"Coz he's a fucking animal mate that's why! This is Kenny fucking King of the Dogs of War!" responded Davies, aggressively yet playfully.

"Aw fuck man I didn't realise you were Kenny King, you're a legend in the battalion mate."

The Sgt realised very quickly that some of these men had known each other quite some time and didn't want to ruffle feathers on their first encounter. Sgt Flowers had only been with the Para's for six months after transferring from 9 Squadron Royal Engineers. He had passed his para training three years previous but on reaching the rank of Sgt decided to transfer in the hope of

113

getting prepared for SAS selection, which he planned to do in the future. Kenny wasn't impressed with his arse kissing and confronted him on it.

"Listen mate, what's your name?"

"I'm Mike Flowers of A Coy."

"Listen up Flowers, I don't need some fucking crap hat Sgt bulling me up and kissing my arse, it's fucking embarrassing when people say shit like that. I'm a paratrooper not Jesus Christ!" he snapped at the Sgt.

"Hey man calm down, I was only trying to get to know you. You are a legend whether you want to be or not, everyone in 2 Para knows who you are. It's good to meet you," he said, leaning towards Kenny with his hand out to shake and calm the situation down.

They shook hands and played cards together for the rest of the day while the men were getting settled into the barracks and getting some bits and bobs from the NAAFI shop on site. The weekend went fast and Monday morning saw the first patrol go out. It was A Coy with support from 1 section of Recce Platoon. They hit the streets of County Antrim and were gone for around four hours when the word came back that the men had come under attack from a riot in one of the main streets. Lt Briar burst into the Sgt's mess screaming.

"Code red, get your riot gear on, the shits hit the fan and the men are trapped on Oriel Road! Let's move!"

Kenny was ready first and he ran to gather his men. They had already started getting ready and into their riot clothing when he arrived.

"Come on lads, let's get the fuck out there and get our men back home safe," shouted Kenny with urgency.

As the men gathered Kenny couldn't help thinking to himself.

"First bloody day in country and it goes tits up."

He smiled to himself as they got into the armoured vehicle and began their drive to the location. Cpl Stevens noticed King smiling.

"What you smiling about?"

Kenny looked Stevens in the eye and responded, "I live for this shit!"

Stevens was shocked, "You're a frickin mad man, I'm just glad you're on my side." he said laughing along at the madness.

They could hear the shouting and crashing of heavy objects as they arrived at the end of the street. They were at the junction with Steeple Road as they de-bussed and got their shields out. Kenny was first to see the gang of men and women pelting rocks at his unprepared friends, who didn't have shields and were taking injuries.

"Two section move your arses now!" he screamed and the men quickly got into formation and began the fast walk down the road towards the rioters.

One of the men turned to see eight men in riot gear coming towards them from behind, they were moving fast and he had a large rock in his hand. He threw it and shouted to his colleagues.

"They're coming from behind us the dirty British feckers!"

The rock fell short and Kenny called the command to charge. He screamed his war cry as if he were in a war type situation. The rioters didn't know what to make of it. Eight men charging a group of maybe forty rioters, they had to be crazy. As the rocks poured down on 2 section the men of A Coy and 1 section were able to gather themselves and their wounded and start to pull back towards the other Steeple Road. It was a minor road compared to the one they were currently on and two armoured vehicles had managed to make their way to the junction ready to pick up the casualties. In the mean time C Coy had also arrived and now thirty armed paratroopers came charging down the street in aid of the cornered patrol. When they arrived they could see 2 section battling it out in an all out fight with the locals. Kenny led his men with ferocity.

Kenny was hit in the head by a baseball bat. He felt his brain rattle inside his helmet as the bat struck him a second and third time. He swung his right fist wildly out in front of himself hoping to connect with the rioter. It did. It caught the man just under the chin ripping his head backwards knocking the man out cold.

Kenny stood on the felled man as he lunged

forward at the next attacker. His men were thrashing out with their riot sticks and spraying mace into the rioters faces. As the other paratroopers arrived the offenders soon fled, leaving a few of their wounded behind to the wrath of 2 Para. A woman came charging towards Lance Cpl Bell from behind but Kenny intercepted her as she got close. He slammed his left fist hard into her face spinning her in mid air as she tumbled backwards into a somersault. It was a vicious punch and he didn't seem to care that it was a female attacker.

"Fucking bitch!" he called out as he hit her.

She lay motionless on the cold damp ground as Bell turned around.

"Thanks boss," Bell shouted with relief.

Two section gathered their men and returned to base leaving C Coy to take care of the mess and carry out aggressive patrolling. This basically meant if anyone tried anything they would go in hard and fast without mercy to prove a point, they were here for the next six months and nobody should underestimate them.

An hour after returning back to barracks Lt Briar called a de-brief meeting in the main mess hall. Alongside Briar was Lt Colonel Hancock of Para HQ Battalion of Aldershot and he didn't look impressed.

"Gents let's get this show on the road, its day one on the streets and we took a heavy hit out there. It was unexpected but we responded with force and dealt with the situation fast and managed to bring our guys back in quickly and relatively safely. The Lt Colonel here would like to raise some issues from today's retaliation. Sir."

He handed the floor over to the Lt Colonel. "Gentlemen," he growled, "I don't think I can call you lot by that title, you're fucking animals!" he screamed getting louder with each word. "I have never seen such an overreaction of force in all my years in the military and I will not accept this kind of behaviour. You assaulted men, women and probably children as if it was a pub brawl. What do you have to say for yourselves?" he demanded as he looked at the senior NCO's.

All three Sgts stood up, King, Flowers and Davies but King spoke first.

"Sir if I may speak on behalf of 2 section?" he asked.

"Speak!" the Lt Colonel snapped.

"Sir we arrived at location to find our men pinned down without any shields or armoured support being pelted with rocks, bricks and bottles. I ordered my section in immediately as I was concerned for the lives of the trapped men. We acted within the boundaries of a full scale riot protocol and dealt with the threat swiftly and effectively."

"Did you indeed?" he snarled, "And what would have happened if the rest of C Company hadn't arrived Sgt? What do you think the casualties would have been then?"

"We handled the situation, Sir, we would have waited until the casualties were out and then withdrawn," he answered confidently.

"We'll never know will we? Let me make one thing clear to you all, you are here because it is your turn to be here, not because we need you here. I will be overseeing this battalion for the next three months and I don't want to see that kind of reaction again, do I make myself perfectly clear?"

"Yes Sir," came the response from the masses and the Lt Colonel left the room.

Lt Briar stood looking on at his men, they were battered and bruised from yet another battle and they looked pissed off at what the Lt Colonel had just said.

"Okay lads now that he's gone I just want to say a huge well done to you all. King you're an absolute madman for going in without backup and that did piss me off. But you got the job done as usual and that's what counts. I'm fucking proud of you all for getting the men out of there."

He turned and walked away feeling proud of his troops but knew if another riot occurred, which it was likely to, then their aggressiveness would not be tolerated unless completely justified.

Over the next three months Sgt King led his men during no less than six full scale riots, three minor disturbances and three field reconnaissance operations. He was proud of his team and Briar and Silvers were suitably impressed with his leadership skills. But as usual it was always in the teeth of battle where he seemed to shine; he truly was a dog of war and lived up to the name with little effort.

During one of the field reconnaissance Op's Kenny and his section were laying up in a hedgerow doing an observation on a disused farm. The British suspected it was being used as a weapons cache by PIRA (Provisional Irish Republican Army). They had been there just over three hours when a dark blue Ford Transit van came hurtling down the country lane before slamming its brakes on hard some five feet past their OP (observation post). King and the others thought they had been rumbled and were about to be confronted. They sat dead still holding their breaths waiting for the attack to present itself.

After being parked up for around two minutes a shot was fired in the back of the van and the back doors swung open. The troop's bodies bolted into a rigid state of shock waiting for the inevitable. A body was thrown to the ground and the van sped off again as the men in the back struggled to close the doors.

The body was battered and bloody. Kenny radioed HQ and they gave him permission to break cover and recover the body. An Army ambulance was on route along with an APC (Armoured Personnel Carrier) to pick up his section. Kenny crawled out of the hide under the hedgerow and moved toward the body. The tout (a name given to an Irish spy who collaborates with the British) had been beaten and tortured and finally shot in the head at close range. Despite his condition he was recognised by Cpl Stafford as a local tout who'd been working for the British for over two years. Stafford had done a three month secondment with Pathfinder Platoon the year before and was told to leave this guy alone as he was a key player in PIRA and therefore invaluable to the Green Slime (The Army Intelligence Corps).

When they arrived back at base Kenny was told that the tout had been missing for eight days. By the looks of this guy he'd been tortured for the full duration. The Irish were renowned for their brutality when it came to traitors and this was no exception.

Kenny left Ireland and completed his Senior Command Course earning his rightful rank of Sergeant and finally got his pay rise. He did find the course tough but came near the top of his class, as he had done previously on the Junior Command Course. He returned to Colchester barracks a couple of days before the unit got back from NI and was looking forward to catching up with his friends, especially Black as they hadn't had much time to hang out since the promotion.

He was sitting in the NAAFI bar having a quiet pint of larger when Company Sergeant Major

(CSM) WO2 Mann walked up to him and snatched the newspaper out of his hands. Kenny leapt to his feet ready to punch the lights out of him when he realised who it was.

"Hey there, calm the fuck down young King," the CSM laughed and Kenny smiled at him.

They had known each other since Kenny joined 2 Para seven years ago. Gerry Mann was a tough bastard and an old school Para who took no shit from anyone, that's how he got to the position he did at such a young age. He had made the rank of WO2 (Warrant Officer 2nd class) at the age of twenty nine and CSM of 2 Para at age thirty one. Kenny was glad to see him after all this time.

"Bloody hell Gerry! How longs it been?"

"Last time I saw you, you were heading out to Africa. How long ago was that?" he asked shaking his head. "I never thought I'd see the day you'd be wearing three stripes, ya crazy fool."

"Wow has it been that long mate? That was eighteen months ago, I didn't actually apply for the job to be honest mate. It was just kind of given to me as a trial and then the next thing I knew I was back in The Shot (Aldershot) doing my seniors course."

"Yeah I know, that's how I heard you were back from Ireland. Sounds like you guys had a rough time out there, a few nasty injuries."

"Yeah we had a couple of guys from A Coy medivaced out after the first patrol coz of some damaged tendons in the leg, or something like that and one of our guys too. Do you remember Tony Bowers?"

He nodded, "Yeah tall skinny fella, too big to be a Para but they let him through coz he was a real tough nut. Is that him, a cockney fella?" the CSM asked quizzing King.

"Yep that's the one, he stood up and let loose with a dozen plastic bullets but the rifle jammed and he got hit in the chest with a breeze block breaking six ribs. He couldn't breathe properly so the medics had to pierce his chest to release the pressure off his heart and lungs. He was in a bad way mate. Yet he pulled through and stayed on doing some bullshit admin role rather than being sent back. I think he was scared they'd give him a medical discharge if he came back without the boss."

"Yeah but there's been two badly injured in the last month hasn't there?" the CSM asked.

"Has there?"

Kenny looked concerned because he hadn't heard from his men in the last two or three weeks, he just put it down to them being busy and the Sgt who was put in charge was his new friend, Sgt Flowers.

"Aw shit Kenny, I thought you knew. Bob Moore is in hospital in London, he took two rounds in his right leg. They've saved the leg but he's in a bad way from losing so much blood and they're not sure he'll be able to stay in." He paused allowing Kenny to digest what was being said to him. "Then

123

a new guy stood on a land mine and blew his balls off. Survived for what it was worth."

"Holy fuck who was that?" Kenny asked, shocked at the news.

"Lance Cpl Bond was his name; he was one of yours wasn't he?" The CSM could see he was distressed by the news and waited patiently for him to look at him. "Kenny are you okay?"

"Yeah mate I'm fine, but that poor bastard had only joined us two months before Ireland. He was a decent kid with bags of potential, that's a real shame." Kenny sank back into his chair in disbelief. "How the fuck did he miss a landmine? Was it in the field or on the streets?"

"I dunno mate, listen you'll get all that info when the boys get back. They're not your section when you're not there. They were with an experienced guy from A Coy I think, when it happened."
The CSM said trying to reassure him.

"Experienced my arse! He's a fucking hat who's only been in the regiment six months! He tried crawling up my arse telling me how great I was and all that bollocks. I could have fucking slapped him but I was on trial for my stripe. I can't believe he didn't see a landmine, we did loads of training on this shit."

"Okay Kenny that's enough, I'll tell you what happened but you drop this act now and get on with the job in hand, agreed?" Mann ordered.

"Okay, okay," King agreed.

"They were just getting out of the field after a low

risk op, a bit of observation. They came sauntering down the hillside to the pickup vehicle when some bloke from the engineers shouted over to him. They were old mates who hadn't seen each other for a while, I guess he thought he was home free so he cut across the field and stepped on a felled tree stump and it was wired with two British issue grenades and they blew his balls off and some of his thighs too. He's in a bad way Kenny and they're not sure if he's going to make it. He's in a paddy hospital coz he's too weak to move."

"Holy shit Gerry I can't believe it. So it wasn't really anybody's fault then?"

"No definitely not mate; it was just pure bad luck."

Kenny spent the next few days in camp with his friends and had a good drink with his old buddy Richard Black. He then requested a flight pass to go visit Bond in hospital but by the time he arrived at the hospital the bad news had arrived, he was just pulling up outside the hospital doors when his phone rang.

"I'm just outside now, so I'll be there in a minute or two," said King to the Doctor on the other end of the line.

"I'm sorry Sgt King but Mr Bond died a few moments ago, we couldn't resuscitate him. I'm sorry," said the Doctor in a sombre tone.

Kenny returned back to the UK on the next flight. As he drifted in and out of consciousness he thought back to his days in basic training, especially P Company. It was without a doubt one of the toughest training assessments in the world and the British Parachute Regiment are known for their toughness.

It was a Tuesday when they fell in on Balloon Square. There stood the CO for P (Pegasus) Company Major John Fisher, his face was battered and worn and looked as if he's had a tough life. He was a championship boxer which was frowned upon by the Army as it wasn't very dignified for officers to partake in such sports. Next to him stood WO2 Company Sgt Major (CSM) Warner, he had been part of the P Company team for fourteen years, the longest serving member in history and a legend in the regiment. One of the fittest, toughest old bastards ever to walk the earth as far as his men were concerned, he had served for twenty two years and the regiment had extended his contract for a further three due to his expertise and ability to get the right men through training, or get rid of those he didn't believe should be in his beloved regiment. He didn't look much physically, he was medium build with mousy brown hair with flecks of grey in the sides; he wasn't overly muscular but his confidence and strong body language said it all. He was supremely fit and renowned for his ability to mould the young men of recruit training.

The recruits of 402 platoon stood to attention. They were wearing full fighting order, a

Bergen weighing a minimum of 35lbs not including water bottle, their Self Loading Rifle (SLR) and were getting prepared for the first of eight tests to earn their red beret. The 10 mile speed march was a real ball breaker and several recruits tended to fall on this test alone. They were given 1 hour 50 minutes to complete the course and they had to complete it as close to a full platoon as possible, however the platoon usually stretched out over a couple of miles due to the men's varying fitness levels despite them all receiving the same basic training.

It was week twelve, it was cold and there was rain in the air as they were given the order to move out. Along with the Major and the CSM there were eight Sgts and four Cpls assisting the team, two of which were medics who would keep an eye on the recruits to ensure they were fit to continue rather than fit to drop. The other two were PTI's (Physical Training Instructors). Only the best Sgt's across 5 Airborne Brigade were selected and invited to be part of P Company; it was a huge honour to be asked to join its ranks.

CSM Warner began, "Right gents its show time and I don't want any faggots in my regiment, so if you're a queer you can piss off now before you fake your collapse at around the five mile mark. We've seen it all before ladies so don't fucking bother. Remember excuses are like arse holes, everyone's got one. Now let's do it, forward march, left, right, left, right, left, right, left."

Kenny was in the third row of men from the front, there were thirty men in total on the march on this day but he felt confident that he would complete this test without any major problems. They marched for a few hundred yards before breaking into double time, the heavy pack on their backs soon started to rub and bounce on those who failed to secure everything tight enough. King's kit was solid, he had spent a lot of time preparing for this moment with his roommate and now close friend Brian Coleman. Coleman was another Yorkshire man who had joined at the same time as King and they ended up sleeping side by side. They often talked about nights out in Leeds and as Coleman was from Barnsley he talked about the girls he'd slept with from Sheffield, Huddersfield and most of South Yorkshire. If it moved he'd shagged it, according to his stories. But they always got a good laugh from the other recruits which helped lighten the mood on the tough days, which was most days.

The march had being going for around an hour and the pace seemed to quicken as they hit the tank tracks for a second time. The recruit boots slipped and slid as they sank into the deep clay. The ground was made up of a mixture of sand, rocks and thick mud which gave way under your feet as you climbed each hill. Kenny leaned into the hill as he charged up it for a second time. He was breathing heavily and sweat streamed down his face, his red T-shirt was stuck to him from the light drizzle and sweat. His mind was screaming "no more, I can't take it" but his legs carried on putting one foot in front of the other.

As he got to the top of the hill Sgt Miller was standing there shouting and balling at the recruits.

"Get a fucking move on, the war will be over by the time you girls get there. King, move your fat arse up that hill and get moving or you've no chance of passing this first time around."

King suddenly felt panic grip him as he thought.

"What if he's telling the truth and I'm already behind on the time to complete the course."

When under stress and feeling exhausted he had failed to realise that he was near the front of the field so if he was failing then so was everyone else and that just couldn't be possible. In fact Kenny crossed the line sprinting in order to beat his roommate Coleman who came up behind him shouting.

"I'm going to beat you, ya fat bastard!"

Kenny gave it everything he had in order to beat his friend and he did by about two feet. The CSM was delighted to see such camaraderie and determination. They had passed in a time of 1 hour and 32 minutes.

"Well done King, Coleman. Get away and get cleaned up, drink plenty of fluids and get some hot scoff down ya."

Chapter 8

Reconnaissance Platoon were gathering their gear and heading to Brize Norton in Oxfordshire, this was home of the RAF jump school and was always a welcome treat, as the standards of food and accommodation were much better than that of the Army. They were there for three days and the intention was for them to get at least four mandatory jumps in (and possibly the eight that were required each year for Recce) to ensure the men of 2 and 3 Para maintained their active Para competency.

1 Para were only expected to do two jumps every two years, which is why they were considered the soft part of the regiment, when in fact there was no soft part to the Parachute Regiment. All of the men were highly trained, some of the best infantry soldiers in the British Army. Plus there were big plans on the horizon for 1 Para and their active role in the future of the Special Forces (SF) in the UK. Only the top brass were aware of the plans at this time, so other battalions didn't get wind of this and try to leave 2 and 3 Para to head for 1 Para placements, in the hope of getting active service with the SF.

The first day was perfect; the weather was bright sunshine with ground temperatures of around 25 degrees with hardly a cloud in the sky. This was a good jump day. The Para Jump Instructor (PJI) decided to get a Hercules C130 and have all three sections do the jump together; they piled into the cold metal frame and sat in the fuselage waiting for take-off and chatted amongst themselves. Once up in the air they prepared for the jump, standing up and checking the man in the front to ensure his chute was packed correctly and there were no loose straps etc.

The red light came on, which was the sign to move into position.

"Three minutes Sir," called the Jump Master, who was now opening the doors on both sides of the plane.

Lt Briar called the command back and it was passed down the line to the last man. They shuffled with the weight of their laden Bergen's across their knees and rifle strapped across the Bergen. The Lt stood in the doorway on the left side of the plane as its engines roared. Lt Briar would lead the left stick and Sgt Davies the right stick, once they hit the drop zone (DZ) they had to pack up their gear and TAB (Tactical Advance to Battle) the 10 miles back to Brize Norton.

There were a bunch of recruits sitting on board with them, hoping to get a feeling of what it would be like when they got to that part of their training. They had just passed P Company and the RSM of Para Depot decided it would be a good motivator. He was right; they looked on in awe at the men of 2 Para's Recce Platoon as they prepared to jump. They didn't sit quietly like they did in recruit training, as there was little fear for most of these hardened veterans, it seemed a long time since they were recruits.

The Jump Master shouted, "Stand by! Ten seconds."

He paused as the countdown came and went in what seemed to last much longer, the green light came on and he screamed at the Lt and his men.

"Red on, Green on. Go! Go! Go!"

The men threw themselves out of the door one after another without hesitation. Kenny was at the back of the right stick and after his chute had deployed and he'd checked everything was okay, he looked below and noticed one of the team members chutes hadn't fully deployed. He could see one half of the chute flapping about as the trooper plummeted downwards at speed. There wasn't anything he could do about it but watch.

The man attached to the chute was Private Tony Bowers, he had looked up to see some of his rig tangled and unopened. Instead of floating down at around 20 mph he was heading for the ground at 40 mph. The chance of surviving without injury was low and he knew he had to do something about it quickly. After numerous attempts to correct his chute he gave up and cut away his rifle and equipment to slow him down before hitting the quick release button on the front of his harness and the chute flew from his body. As he continued to fall he pulled at the reserve chute handle but nothing happened. He tried again before realising it was futile and with that thought he relaxed and accepted the inevitable.

As he hit the ground his spine snapped in three places, his left leg doubled up and came away from the hip. The leg was pointing in the same direction as his head before it hit the ground, coming apart, brains spilling out onto the cold rocky floor. Blood was everywhere! Tony Bowers was 23 years old; he hit the ground at around 50 mph and died on impact. The military ambulance had already been notified to be at the DZ and they pronounced him dead on arrival.

The other men watched in horror as their friend died hitting the ground. The impact occurred just six feet away from Cpl Steve Taylor, a friend and section member who had known him for over four years. After dealing with the incident Lt Briar decided to call the exercise off and arranged for a couple of trucks to collect the soldiers. The Lt called his SNCO's over for a debrief while the other soldiers got into the vehicles and headed back to camp.

"Gents this has been a day of tragedy and there will of course be a full investigation. However I have two people I am really concerned about and that is Cpl Taylor who Bowers almost landed on and Private Newland who checked his pack when in line on the aircraft," Lt Briar looked around at his men as he awaited their response.

"Unbelievable," said Sgt Davies, "I've known that kid since he joined us a few years back, he was a good lad and he didn't deserve to go like this after everything we've been through."

"Yeah it's been a rough day for everyone I reckon, let's just get back and have a piss up on his behalf," responded Sgt Fisher.

"Sir with all due respect we've got jumps booked in all day and I think the best thing we can do it get them back up there before they start thinking about things too much. What do you think boss?" said Kenny.

"Yes I know Kenny but it's a bit harsh, don't you think, to make them jump after this?" responded Lt Briar.

"He's right you know," said Davies, "the last thing we want is this lot going to mush tomorrow when they've had time to think about it."

"Fuck man I don't know, if I had it my way we'd ditch the whole week and head back to camp and bring them back another time," said Fisher looking amazed that they were considering another jump today.

"Oh fuck it your right King, we can't waste thousands of pounds in resource on a perfect jumping day and allow the men to think about it any longer than they have to," the Lt said with conviction.

They jumped into the Land Rover and drove back

to camp, then went off to speak to their sections. Lt Briar called Major Silvers to tell him the bad news and explained his plan to continue with the jumps. Kenny arrived at the barracks and gathered him men around.

"Listen up men, the day isn't over yet. We've got three more jumps to get in today and what happened doesn't change anything," said Kenny.

"You're fucking kidding me aren't you boss? We've just watched one of our own go fucking squish on the ground and you expect us to go back up and throw ourselves out the door again!" shouted Lance Cpl Stollers.

"You can cut that shit out right now Cpl or I'll knock you the fuck out here and now. We're Paras and we fight on when all else around us goes to shit. I'm gutted about Bowers but that's life and it's a risk we take every time we saddle up and make a jump." Snapped Sgt King making sure they remembered who was in charge.

Cpl Stafford spoke up, "Sgt I think the guys would rather take today off to get over the incident first, that's all. They don't mean any disrespect."

"Nicely put," said Private Sanders and the others agreed with nodding of their heads and murmurs of approval.

"Oh really, so when we were under heavy fire in Africa and I was wearing Private Brice's brains all over my face, you think I should have stopped and said, can you wait a minute while I gather myself? Are you lot fucking kidding me? I wasn't asking

135

you if you fancied going for a drive and a picnic. I am telling you that we're jumping today and that's the fucking end of it. So get your shit together and get prepared to jump at least another three times today."

He turned his back and stormed out to get his own gear ready for the flight. The men reluctantly got ready and fell in outside, the SNCO's waited with Lt Briar. Briar stepped forward to speak to his men.

"I know most of you are thinking that we're crazy for making you do this considering what happened, but you need to learn that if you pack your chute incorrectly this kind of thing will happen eventually. Without being too disrespectful of the dead, Bowers was told on numerous occasions as far back as basic to get his shit in order and I'm sure the investigation will find something similar has happened here today. You will all jump today because we are Paratrooper's and this is what we do in the face of adversity, it's time to man up, good luck." He turned and walked over to the aircraft and the Sgts instructed their men to do the same. They jumped another four times that day and once during the night getting in six of the eight jumps they were expected to.

After their time at Brize Norton they returned to Colchester and prepared for a night on the town. Most units stuck to their own rank when they went out, Privates and Lance Corporals together, Junior

NCO's in another bar or area of town. Senior NCO's in another and Officers in another world altogether but in Recce Platoon it was different. The ranks still had their own bar and club on site and still went to the same haunts as the other equivalent ranks but they also went out as a unit. This ensured the team worked well together no matter what the situation.

They entered the first bar of the night and Sgt Davies went to the bar with his section in tow and called the order to the bar maid. "I'll have six pints of Fosters and two pints of Guinness love when you're ready," he said winking at the young girl working behind the bar.

She was average to look at but quite sweet and attractive because of it. Five feet five inches tall, pale skin and black hair with the biggest deep brown eyes he had ever seen, but at age eighteen she was a little too young for Sgt Davies to make a play at her. This didn't stop his men from trying their luck, unsuccessfully.

Kenny moved to the right hand side of the bar where an older lady was serving, she was obviously an experienced bar maid due to the way she served and bantered with the lads of all ages. Brenda knew how to get her tips, with her low cut top showing her heaving bosoms and skirt showing her shapely legs.

The younger girl Emma wore a simple pair of black pants and a well fitting black T-shirt which gave very little away other than the fact that she had a reasonable figure. Kenny called Brenda over and ordered a round for his section and then moved to a standing area in the middle of the pub so they could watch the ladies, as well as what was going on in the bar. They were always alert and watching out for trouble. It became habit after a while. They would sit with their backs against the wall in bars and restaurants to ensure they could see if anything out of the ordinary was coming at them and would plan an escape route should it be needed.

The night went on and the drinking got heavy. Kenny was drinking pints of Stella Artois as if they were going out of fashion. He had just finished his tenth pint when a scuffle broke out near the bar. Private Sanders had been getting a round in when he noticed a pretty girl behind him, so he began to chat with her and she reciprocated. He figured he was in with a chance. Unfortunately for the girl, her boyfriend turned up behind her as they were chatting and realised that she was in fact giving Jason the come on.

The guy was tall and heavy set, so the first punch knocked Sanders off his feet, but he jumped back up so fast his back hardly hit the ground. The tray of beer went everywhere and Sanders ran at the guy throwing everything he had at him, unfortunately Sanders was no match for this guy's size and he started to get the better of him.

Kenny grabbed the attacker by the scruff of

his neck, dragging him off Sanders with his left hand while throwing a heavy blow to the man's kidneys with his right fist, knocking the wind out of him. He gasped for air as Kenny began to unleash a devastating array of punches to his body and head. The guys eyes were almost closed from the swelling and his nose splattered across his face. Kenny barely broke a sweat and as he stopped hitting this guy another came at him. Kenny caught the attackers arm and threw him over his shoulder; he came crashing to the ground. Kenny smiled at him before speaking.

"If I were you sunshine, I'd take your boyfriend and fuck off out of here before I really lose my temper," he said softly but firmly. He stood up and called to the rest of the guys, "let's get the fuck out of here men, it's full of gays and lady boys!"

A couple of weeks went by with them all going through the usual routine, Kenny's section was training hard, doing long runs, circuits, weapons training and tabbing at least twice a week. The other Sgts watched on as he drove his men harder than any of the other sections. The whole platoon was due to go on exercise on Salisbury Common the following week and Kenny was excited about it. It was his chance to show the brass what he had done with his new section. He ordered his men to stay off the piss that weekend to ensure they were in top physical shape when they jumped on the Monday night.

139

They carried out the night jump onto the common without a hitch at 2300 hours and went into an all round fighting position, while they waited for Sgt King to reach them. He ran over in the monkey run with his Bergen on his back and gave the order to move into the woods, they were to set up a perimeter around what would become the command post (CP) for the officers while in the field.

Once the CP was set up and the officers had got into position, his section was sent out to carry out a Recce mission lasting approximately 48 hours. When they returned they passed all intelligence to the CP and a team was chosen to carry out an attack on the enemy position.

The men of 2 section had built their hides during the night and laid up most of the day observing a cottage in the middle of nowhere. They gathered every single piece of information such as, how many people came and went and at what times, what were they wearing, did they have weapons and if so what kind etc.

Once they had relayed the info to the CP Kenny waited impatiently to see if they would get the go ahead to launch the attack. When Lt Briar sent 1 section in to carry out the attack, Kenny was totally pissed off. He needed the action and missed the adrenaline rush of battle. He lay in his bivi and fell asleep in a bad mood and began to dream about his childhood. The dreams were scattered and didn't make much sense, they were more like clips in a movie flashing through his mind in black and white.

He remembered his mother's boyfriend Tim, coming home from the pub on Saturday night and knocking his mum around thinking he was a tough guy. He turned on Kenny on several occasions, punching him in the head and kicking him to the body when he fell to the floor.

"Come on ya fat bastard, ya fucking retard, get up and fight like a man," Tim shouted.

"A man, a fucking man," yelled his mother, "what kind of man hits a woman and her son you fucking coward? One of these days you'll get what's coming, you wait and see."

That night Tim beat Kenny's mother within an inch of her life. She was in hospital for over a month and Kenny suffered two broken ribs and a fractured cheek bone. Tim was arrested but his mother refused to press charges for fear of him getting away with it and coming after them again. The good thing was that she left him and they never saw him again. They were in the town centre one day when his mum bumped into an old friend of hers who knew Tim quite well.

"I know you're probably not interested in gossip about Tim but have you heard what happened to him?" asked the friend.

"No luv, what's happened?" she asked.

"He was hit by a bus just down the road there. He was pissed and started knocking his girlfriend about in the middle of the street and she pulled a knife out and went for him. As he jumped backwards a bus was coming down the street at around 20 mph and hit him side on, smashing him up. Then the driver drove over him and finished him off. Terrible tragedy don't you think?"

"Ha ha ha ha," laughed his mum, "I've never heard such good news in my life! Oh I know you think I'm being a bitch but you weren't on the receiving end of those punches and you didn't have to watch him beat your eight year old son half to death."

She screamed at her friend who looked at her with horror.

"No I don't suppose I do. I guess I just didn't expect you to laugh about it, that's all," she looked like she wanted to get out of there quickly so his mother gave her the excuse she needed.

"Well I can't stand around here all day gassing; we've got to get on. You take care of yourself and if you see his family tell them to burn in hell from me," she smirked as she walked away from the woman.

An explosion woke Kenny from his sleep! He grabbed his gear and ran to gather his men. The attack hadn't exactly gone to plan and the enemy were ready for the attackers. They let loose with mortars and UGL's on M16's, they were well equipped and well organised, just as he had warned the CP only hours earlier. The exercise lasted two days and included attacks, defences and field craft training delivered by the SAS and the de-brief was held outside the CP while they awaited the trucks to return them to camp.

While the officer talked, Kenny found himself drifting off, his attention was somewhere else when Major Silvers noticed and called him to answer a question.

"Isn't that right Sgt King? Could you give us your assessment of the situation?" he asked, waiting for Kenny to suffer the embarrassment of not knowing what he was talking about.

"Yes Sir it is, I warned the CP only two hours prior to the attack about the type of weapons being carried in and out of the cottage and that the men looked fit and well built, which told me that this wasn't going to be no push over, Sir."

Kenny smiled at the Major, acknowledging his disappointment that he was in fact listening to some of it and this was usually enough for him to take in the majority of what was being said.

After the de-brief they went back to camp and got cleaned up, Kenny was disappointed that he was unable to get more involved in the exercise. He started to realise just how much he missed the real action and wondered if he was normal for thinking this.

He returned from an 18 mile run as a camp runner (someone who runs errands around camp) caught up with him.

"Excuse me Sgt, can I just confirm that you're Sgt

King?"

"Yes I'm Sgt King, what is it?" asked Kenny.

"Major Silvers has called all the Junior and Senior NCO's to an urgent briefing about 20 minutes ago and has demanded that I find you and get you there pronto. His words Sgt," he said waiting to be bollocked for relaying the order.

King followed the runner to the Officers mess, which surprised him as they never held briefings there. As he got to the door the RSM was waiting, looking angry at King's tardiness.

"Where the fuck have you been?" demanded the RSM.

"Shopping, where does it look like I've been?" he responded sarcastically, "I've been for a run."

"Well you're fucking late for an urgent briefing, now get your arse in there and sneak in at the back. Here's my notebook and pen so you can take some info down," he said ushering him along.

As he attempted to sneak into the back of the lecture hall, Major Silvers noticed him sitting down.

"Nice of you to join us Sgt King, you have missed the first fifteen minutes of the intro so I will quickly tell you what's going on. In short we're going to Somalia to work with Pathfinder Platoon and take out a team of guerrillas, who are holding captive three British nationals. Once we're done there we'll be heading back to North Africa to finish what we left undone last time. General Gooder is kicking some serious arse over there and we need to take him out once and for all."

He carried on providing the tactical formations and other vital info required for the operation and then asked the three Sgts to hang back, as the others left.

"There is a slight change of plan on this one gents, I'd like King to lead 3 section if that's okay with you Sgt Davies?" he asked, although it wasn't really a question.

"No problem Sir, may I ask why the change Sir?" Davies asked.

"Two section are in top condition but you've got new bods in there as well as another Private joining you today who won't have a fucking clue what's going on. King has proved that he is good at taking this kind of challenge on and I want him to run with it. You will have 3 section and after seeing their standards I have no doubt you will be impressed with their professional ability, any problems Sgt?"

"No Sir, I'll get the men together and explain the situ to them now," he left the room and went straight to the barracks to pass on the info and get the men ready.

Davies knew that King's men were top notch and would already be getting their kit together. He spoke to the men and explained. Although most were disappointed to be losing their Sgt of two years, Black was ecstatic about getting his buddy back.

The men flew out to Somalia landing in Mogadishu, Aden Adde International Airport. They were immediately loaded up into military trucks and driven to their temporary barracks; it was like an old tin shed which had obviously been used for farming in the past. It had straw beds on the floor with dirty grey sheets spread over them and the soldier showing them to their quarters seemed to think they should have been impressed. The men took one look and started to moan and groan at the standard of accommodation they would be living in for the next couple of weeks.

"Fuck me Kenny, couldn't you find anywhere worse for us to stay? This is just too good for us," Black said sarcastically.

"Quit your moaning, we've been back together five fucking minutes and you're already bitching. This is as good as it gets. We've slept in worse so cut the shit and get your gear prepared to go out tonight," King responded.

The three sections of men split the living accommodation so they could discuss each role without getting involved or confused by the other sections order. Sgt Davies was getting to know the guys in his section and Kenny was enjoying being back with his old section again. One and three sections would be going out on a Recce tonight with 2 section staying back in reserve. Davies hoped the others didn't get into any trouble. That way his men could get a good night's sleep and be prepared for their recce the following night.

King and Fisher lead their men into the night, Mogadishu was a hostile place with eyes everywhere and the militia wasted no time coming down heavy on intruders in their neighbourhood. It was King's third time in the country so he knew some of the streets and the hot spots to avoid quite well. The two sections slipped into the night and gathered as much Intel as they could on the team of guerrillas who were holding the British hostages. They had managed to identify which building the guerrillas were staying in which meant the prisoners couldn't be far away. Probably in the cellar as this was a regularly used scenario for such an operation.

The teams made it back without being detected before sunrise. The men were exhausted from the heat of the night. It was around twenty eight degrees and was set to be a hot day in the tin shed. King and Fisher debriefed the officers and 2 section and then stayed on guard duty until 0700 hours, before they ate supper and grabbed some sleep while 2 section stayed on day light guard duty.

King drifted off quickly and began to dream again, this time he was on his first draft in NI. It was a tough tour with lots of riots and killings; he was a little shocked by it all but felt the urge to get involved whenever possible. He remembered seeing one of his oppo's shot in the neck by an IRA sniper. He survived but ended up with a voice box for the rest of his life and needless to say he was discharged from the Army.

He thought about the days on patrol in Belfast and the stints in the outposts of South Armagh. He hated it the first time he went but became quite fond of it once he joined Recce platoon. In recce he spent most of his tour in the field which was where he was most comfortable. Several higher ranks had told him at the time that he had the makings of a sniper, a course which he later took and passed with relative ease. It is a tough course run by the battalions, soldiers sometimes sent off to another regiment or Corps to train them up.

Kenny woke up to the smell of fresh coffee and wondered where he was. He lifted his head to see Private Black making a brew on his stove and the other men in his section cleaning weapons and eating their rations. The ration packs had come a long way since he joined the Army. They used to be dry or tinned foods that where tough to swallow, where as now they were like camping meals where you simply placed the bag of food into boiling water, or you could eat them cold if need be. He sat up and Black passed his friend the cup of coffee smiling at him.

"What the fuck you so happy about?" asked King feeling exhausted.

"I can't believe how long you've been asleep mate, your normally last one asleep and first one up.

148

You must be shattered!" said Black.

"I am mate, how long have I been asleep?" he asked as he looked at his watch.

"Six hours mate, like I said it's been a long time since I've seen you sleep like that."

Kenny opened up his Bergen and got his rations out, meat balls and pasta. He smiled at the thought of the tasty treat, it was his favourite and he couldn't wait to get it down him. He heated some water and boiled the bag for twenty minutes so it was piping hot, once done he shovelled the meal down and felt the warmth passing through his body with every mouthful.

Major Silvers walked into the shed and the men began to stand up as a sign of respect.

"As you were men," he said putting them at ease.

"It looks like they could be getting ready to move out so we may have to go in tonight. Davies as your team hasn't had chance to recce the place it's probably best that you stay at the back in reserve. Sgt Fisher will lead the assault and Sgt King; you will lead the rescue mission. Let's get in and out as fast as we can without anyone getting hurt, on our side anyway," he said mischievously.

Kenny watched his men getting ready and noticed the new guy. Private Brown seemed a little tense. He walked over to him and sat down as he packed his gear.

"Hey Brown, how's it going? Are you settling into the team okay?" asked Kenny.

"Yeah Sgt I'm fine thanks, I guess when I joined

recce I thought I'd get some training before going out on a live Op but this is what I joined for so I've just got to man up and get on with it," he responded sounding nervous.

"There's no shame in being scared Brown, we all go through it in our own way. My first month with recce we got called to Bosnia and I got my first kill. Talk about throw up, man I couldn't stop being sick." He laughed out loud trying to put the Private at ease. "How long you been with the regiment son?"

"Three years Sgt, I came over from 3 Para coz there weren't any places in Recce Platoon over there. When they told me I would be working with the likes of you and Sgt Davies I have to admit I got a bit nervous."

"Nervous," Kenny looked puzzled. "Why on earth would you be nervous about me and Bri?" He asked.

"Because of your reputations, I don't mean to go on Sgt coz I know you probably don't like that shit but you're a fucking legend and Davies is renowned as being one the best Sgt's in the regiment," he said getting excited.

"Well your right we don't like all that shit but thanks anyway. I guess what I'm trying to say to you is don't worry about the Op. Just do what you're trained to do and we'll be in and out in no time, hopefully without anyone getting hurt. I need to ask you though, have you ever killed anyone?" Kenny asked.

"No Sgt, I've fired a few rounds at people in Iraq but I don't think I hit anyone. No confirmed anyway," he spoke, almost disappointed at not getting that first kill under his belt.

"We're off to Niger after this and I can tell you now that you will be getting that confirmed. We have to finish what we couldn't last time and I want to see that fucker burn. We lost a few good men out there, not to mention the fact that they brought a fucking building down on me."

He laughed trying to make light of the situation.

"Thanks Sgt, you've put me at ease and don't you worry about me. When the time comes there'll be no hesitation."

"I know son, let's hope so anyway or we'll be packing you off home in a black bag. You don't get any second chances out there, its do or die shit. Let's get this one done first before we think about the next Op."

They nodded at each other and Kenny went back to getting his own equipment ready, the sections formed up and got ready to move out. They were heavily laden with extra ammo and water in case anything went wrong. They wanted to be prepared, as there was no outside back up to come bail them out if the shit hit the fan.

The Major was right, as 1 section approached the building they could see armed men loading boxes and what looked like an old TV camera from the

80's into two trucks. The two sections got into position ready to carry out the snatch, the good news was that at this rate they wouldn't have to go into the building because the guerrilla troops were about to move the prisoners and take them to a new location. Fisher got his men into place along the outer wall of the building and King took his men around the other side ready to snatch the three British prisoners.

They could hear the muffled moans and groans of people being ushered across the room heading for the front door. The armed men scanned the area as they moved the captives into the street to be loaded into the truck. A tall man popped his head around the corner to see Fisher standing inches from him, Fisher stuck his knife into the man's throat and twisted it left and right. As he fell forward his rifle hit the ground alerting the others and all hell broke loose, the guerrillas began firing wildly at the walls from inside hoping to hit their enemy. Luckily no one was hit and Fisher began to assault the building. Kenny heard the men dragging the screaming people back into the building and couldn't afford to let them barricade themselves in or kill the prisoners.

He planted a small explosive on the wall near the back of the building and stepped aside.
"Fire in the hole," he called to his section.

BOOM! The explosion rocked the building and the street and he knew it would only take minutes for an attack to come from the neighbouring houses. He jumped through the hole in the wall to see two men with rifles standing at the other end of the room next to some stairs leading down to a cellar. He raised his rifle and shot both men in the chest, three shots each. They went down hard, bouncing down the stairs.

"Move," shouted Kenny at his men, "Get those prisoners out of the cellar and watch for more skinnies."

Black and Bell moved to the stairwell and threw down a flash bang (White Phosphorus Grenade) before running down the stairs taking them three at a time. Black dropped to the floor and swung his rifle and head around the bottom corner, seeing three armed men holding the hostages and two others aiming high above him. He immediately put two rounds into the head of the first man followed by a burst of ten rounds into the second. Bell jumped down with his rifle raised and shot one man in the head that was stood a foot or so behind the hostages.

The other two men let go of the hostages and began to fire at the Para's, Bell jumped into a recess in the wall while Black crawled back up the stairs, backwards. Kenny came down the stairs with Brown after providing supporting fire for Fishers team. Kenny got to the bottom and Black spoke to him,

"We've got two skinnies at the back pinning us down," his words barely left his mouth when Kenny made his move.

He swung around the corner with rifle raised and put two rounds into the head of one guerrilla and shouted for the other to drop his weapon. He began to raise it when a shot fired over King's shoulder and hit him in the chest, followed by another three rounds to the abdomen. Kenny turned to see Brown shaking with his rifle in his hands.

"Good lad, now let's grab them and get the fuck out."

He leaned down and grabbed a woman by her arm lifting her to her feet,

"I'm Sgt King from the British Parachute Regiment. We're here to get you out Ma'am, can you walk?"

"Yes I think so," she said trembling.

Black and Bell grabbed the other two prisoners and made their escape via the hole in the wall. The whole assault lasted five minutes but this was all the time the locals needed to put in an attack, luckily they were moving out by the time the first shots were fired. They arrived back at the tin shed to be greeted by British Army trucks ready to take them back to the airport. A helicopter would fly the hostages back to a medical centre in Kenya and from there they would meet the paparazzi and tell the world of their terrible ordeal.

As they drove to the airport, the lady Kenny had picked up spoke to him softly.

"Sgt King wasn't it?" she asked.

"Yes Ma'am, that's right," said Kenny.

"Thank you so much for putting your life at risk to rescue us; I can never thank you enough. I will be mentioning you to the news papers," she said smiling.

"No," he snapped, "Please Ma'am that won't be necessary and we don't really want our names mentioning to the public if that's okay. I'm sure you will be briefed on what to say before you get in front of the cameras Ma'am, he smiled at her trying to put her at ease.

"Oh okay, sorry I didn't mean to alarm you. I just wanted to say thank you."

"You're welcome Ma'am; I hope you feel better soon. You'll be back with your family before you know it."

They arrived at the airport and went their separate ways. The men loaded up in a military aircraft and were flown to Niger where they were met by the men of Pathfinder Platoon and the Mountain Troops of A Squadron, 22 SAS. They moved to the barracks where they had stayed previously and got settled in, it felt somewhat homely to Kenny. He had spent a lot of time in Africa over his years with the regiment and had grown to like it, the thing that kept coming back to his mind was, was it the country he liked or the warfare that it provided him.

Chapter 9

The men of Pathfinder shared the same tent as Recce Platoon and so they got to chatting as Kenny had questions.

"So Sgt Riddle, I thought we were coming to Somalia to help you guys not do your fucking job for you?" said King sarcastically.

"Yeah well who the fuck do you think passed the Intel that they'd moved the hostages numb nuts," he responded laughing.

Kenny and his team laughed along and they chatted and introduced everyone to each other, the following day the SNCO's were called to a briefing with the officers in charge. Major Silvers was there as usual along with the newly promoted Captain Briar, he nodded an acknowledgement at King as he entered the briefing tent.

"Well well well, get you Captain Briar," Kenny mocked.

"Yes Sgt, so watch your arse or you'll be a Cpl again," he responded.

The black humour of the Parachute Regiment isn't readily understood by the outside world and looking in, can appear to be harsh and aggressive but when the going gets tough there is nothing better to break the tension than an inappropriate joke or banter to get things moving again.

The briefing laid out the plans to attack the General's compound. As Recce platoon had been here before they were vital to the Intel provided for the assault. The frontal assault would be led by Sgt Riddle of Pathfinder Platoon while the rear assault would be led by Sgt Davies and 2 section. Kenny had trained them well in CQB (Close Quarter Battle) and had to agree with the decision, after all he'd trained them so he knew how good they were.

King and Fishers sections would be providing covering fire for both assaults while the SAS would attempt to come through the drainage system and plant C4 under the building. As 1 section was a man short they were loaned a sniper who appeared during the briefing, he was Cpl David Josephs of the Royal Marines Commando's (RMC) but that's all they were told or knew about him.

Josephs had been in the Royal Marines for ten years. He had originally selected 42 Commando's K Coy as his first stationing where he spent the first three years of his career before being selected for Recce troop where he spent another three years. He then applied to join the SBS (Special Boat Service) and become part of the Royal Marines Commando's Special Forces. He had trained to be a sniper early in his career with 42 and earned a formidable reputation for the amount of confirmed kills he had racked up.

Despite this reputation he was quite quiet

although always joined in with the banter and could take the piss with the best of them. He had done well on SF selection and after passing the endurance phase he was devastated when he had a panic attack while in the diving phase, which cost him his first chance at becoming an SC3 (Swimmer Canoeist, the initial qualification held by all SBS soldiers). He was returned to his unit and although no one else thought any less of him, he took it very badly and became distant for a while. This was until he was promoted to Cpl and became an S2 (Sniper qualification – All qualifications in the Royal Marines were graded 3, 2 and 1 with 1 being the highest level you could achieve). Josephs decided to excel in the skills he was given and become a sniper first and foremost and would consider his future with the SF later.

It was midnight before they left the compound and headed to the region where General Gooder's complex lay. The Pathfinder's and 1 section shared the lead vehicle, an old Army seven and a half tonner which looked like the rust was holding it together. It was obviously a reject that was used for live firing exercises, by the number of bullet holes it had and some larger holes which had been badly filled with some kind of Polyfilla.

The plan was that 1 section would provide covering fire and backup to the Pathfinder Platoon if needed and the men in the second truck would do the same at the rear of the complex. This included Sgt Davies' 2 section and Sgt King's 3 section, King providing the covering fire and support should it be required. The four men of A Squadron, 22 SAS were going in alone, as they usually did.

Both 1 and 3 sections would be their support should they need it, but in the unlikely event that they failed to plant the explosives and get out successfully they would be trapped in a death tube. Which, if the enemy decided to pour fuel down the hole and set fire to it or if they decided to fire an RPG down there for fun the men of 22 SAS, would be well and truly fucked!

The trucks stopped 5km away from the target location and the men quickly gathered their gear together as the open top Land Rover pulled up behind them. Kenny watched on as the SAS soldiers donned Bergen's the size of Kilimanjaro on top of their webbing and carried their M16's in one hand. They seemed relaxed about the whole thing, as if they didn't have a care in the world. This was what set them apart from everyone else, they were so used to being thrown into combat situations and they accepted death, so they didn't seem to fear it. Or at least that's how it looked on the surface.

One of them walked over to Kenny looking him straight in the eyes.

"Your Kenny King aren't ya?" asked the trooper.

"Yeah that's right," he responded wondering what

was coming next.

"You served with my baby brother a while back over here," he paused for a moment as Kenny looked at him quizzically, "Private Steven Brice," he finished.

"Yeah that's right, he was a cracking lad. It was a real shame mate," Kenny said looking for a reaction. There wasn't one.

"I heard you tried to cover him but these fuckers cut some of your platoon up. Is that right?" He asked sounding a little firmer with his tone.

"We all did our best mate; I don't really remember who did what and when, other than Lance Cpl David Stone. He tried his best before more skinnies came around the corner shooting the shit out of his area. He had to leave your brother to take care of shit and prevent any more kills."

Kenny stopped for a moment while he gauged the situation with this guy.

"So is Stone here today coz I'd like to thank him for what he did or tried to do," he said looking around in the darkness.

"No mate, he died a few months back in another contact. I'm sure he'd just tell you he was doing his job, he was a good lad like that, very modest."

Kenny watched as the guy looked at the ground and for the first time he saw vulnerability.

"Oh well shit happens eh," he changed in a heartbeat into a man of stone cold professionalism.

"I guess so," King responded, surprised at how quickly he could switch off his emotions.

"I'm Bill Brice by the way, the guys call me big Willy but I won't show you why," he said smiling.

They laughed together for a moment before Brice turned away.

"I'll see you on the other side brother," he smiled, turned and walked away.

He looked like a Bergen with legs from the back, his kit weighed around 140lbs but he made it look like he was carrying a picnic bag and heading to the beach with his family. Maybe he was with his family. Kenny got his men together and prepared to move them out.

"We've got 5 clicks to cover in two hours and then we need to be ready to rock and roll by 0300 hours," said Sgt Davies "is that clear?"

"Boss, is it right that the tanks are gonna be backing us up now?" asked Private Hand.

"Yeah the last I heard we've got the Royal Armoured Corps sitting cammed up about 2 clicks away from the complex and if the shit hits the fan they're gonna come in, barrels blazing. So we need to get the fuck out of there if that happens," responded Davies.

By the time the TAB had started the four SAS guys were gone, nowhere to be seen.

"Fuck me Kenny those fuckers must have got a wiggle on to be out of sight already," said Black.

"Yeah they can shift mate that's for sure, they're fit as fuck," Kenny responded to his friend.

"So what did the little fella want with you?" Black asked.

"He was Brice's older brother and he wanted to thank Stone for trying to help him when he got shot."

Black just shrugged his shoulders and smiled, he didn't need to say any more. He knew it would open up old wounds for Kenny, the fact he'd lost a man under his control. They began tabbing at 0015 hours as the weather decided to throw 40 mph winds in their faces and a sprinkling of snow to slow them down.

The one good thing about this weather was that the enemy wouldn't expect the Army to be out there and they certainly wouldn't be expecting an attack from the British after they pulled out so rapidly last time.

General Gooder figured that the British red devils were defeated by his men, so were therefore scared to take on his army again for fear of losing their precious reputation.

Chapter 10

General Gooder sat in his living room talking with his advisors about plans to take on the next region; it was all part of his master plan to eventually take over the whole of Africa. He had delusions of grandeur similar to those ˉof Adolf Hitler. He wanted to be more feared than Hitler and Sadam Hussain put together, he just needed to defeat a reputable regiment like the Para's which he believed he had done previously. This of course served his cause well, small bands of resistance began to disband in reaction to the Para's defeat and despite him losing over 100 of his men he still saw this is a huge victory that would go down in history.

His wife and children also lived in the complex as he felt this was the safest place for them to be. His wife had long thick black hair and big brown eyes and had belonged to an opposing villager's leader at the time he was starting out as a young leader amongst the North African Army. He killed her father in a battle for land and claimed her as his bride shortly after. She didn't resist for fear that her family would be killed, as well as what would have happened to her.

She watched over their two young boys, they were aged eight and six and both had the look of their mother. This pleased Gooder as he felt she had boundless beauty as opposed to his gorilla like features. She was a lighter tone of black that he found attractive and despite the method he used to acquire her, he had fallen madly in love with her and treated her well. He also upheld his promise to look after her family throughout the troubles in Africa, which brought her great respect for him after all he had done in the early days.

His wife and two boys were sitting at the far end of the living room around twenty feet away. The boys were colouring in and drawing pictures of their family when the conversation turned to a more serious note.

"Aduor, take the children out please and prepare a meal for our guests. You will be joining us?" he said as he turned and looked at his military advisors.

"Yes of course Sir." They both responded not daring to turn down the generous offer. "It would be an honour."

She left the room as instructed and the men continued their conversation in private. They were advising Gooder that they had heard that the red devils were planning a return attack to regain their honour and reputation. This made him angry and he jumped to his feet.

"Who do they think they are coming to my country? Imposing on my war! Did they learn nothing of the defeat they took last time? Are they as stupid as people say they are? Obviously they are. Let them come and we will be ready," he bellowed. He continued his rant, "I want new recruits to be sought out as of tomorrow. I want training to be doubled, weapons, hand to hand, weapons and more weapons. Do you understand?" he screamed at the men.

Both men got out their mobile phones and began to make plans. Seeking out new recruits meant truck loads of his men going out into the provinces and taking young boys by force from their families to fight in his army. Anyone who resisted would be killed or tortured in the most gruesome ways.

His head advisor was calling the General's right hand man, Colonel Chibuzo Igwe. Igwe was a brutal man, six feet five inches tall and built like a tank. He was renowned for his brutality around the provinces as well as his tendencies towards young boys. The General turned a blind eye to this due to the fact that he had never let him down. He delivered exactly what his master ordered and would fight to the death for his beliefs.

Chapter 11

It was 0245 hours when the Pathfinders and 1 section arrived at their RV and got into position. The weather had slowed them down, despite it hitting them from the side rather than head on. The attack was due to begin at first light which was 0330 hours and they were already 30 minutes late.

Sgt Riddle got on the radio to speak with Davies. Twenty minutes later he eventually got through.

"What a relief, for a minute there I thought we were well and truly on our own," said Riddle.

"As if I'd let you have all the fun, over." Came Davies response.

Two and 3 sections arrived at the RV at 0305 hours, over an hour late which didn't leave much preparation time. The men immediately got on with eating their rations and cleaning and oiling their weapons.

Sgt Harris of the SAS interrupted the radio conversation bluntly.

"Where the fuck have you arseholes been?"

"I don't know if you noticed but we had a spot of bad weather, over." said Davies.

"No shit, we didn't see any of that coz we were dragging our arses at speed across country to make sure we were in place on time." came the curt response.

166

"Well we're here now so let's get this show on the road," said Riddle.

Kenny took his men to the covering fire positions around the rear of the complex to the North and spread them out in three positions, ten metres apart. The new addition to the team Cpl Jack Rust joined McMann and positioned themselves in one, Black, Bell and Price in another and finally, Harris, Chaplin and Brown. Rust and McMann were solid soldiers who he knew could handle things, but he also wanted to be in a position with a little dead ground behind them so he could move from location to location to provide support if and when needed as well as providing some cover if things went bad.

Kenny watched Davies and his former section moving toward the target. They had to get to within 30 metres of the rear entrance by 0400 hours, the new time which had been set by the SAS due to everyone else being late to the party.

The SAS were already in the drainage system and moved to radio silence. Their only way of communication now was if they were asked a question it was one click on their handset for no, two clicks for yes and three clicks for ask another question.

One section was now in place to the South watching the front gate to the complex and observing the numbers and movements for the rest of the teams. Riddle took his men to within 15

167

metres of the front gate undetected and waited for the signal to attack. The SAS had arranged a tank to come within 800 metres of the East of the complex and fire one round into the wall to distract the enemy soldiers inside.

The Intel had provided them with numbers of around eighty men but Kenny contested this in the briefing, telling them about the underground system they had in place where all the soldiers kept appearing during the last battle. King estimated double this number.

The eighty enemy soldiers were accepted by the briefing but afterwards Sgt Alan Harris called the other SNCO's to a meeting and agreed that King's numbers would be the number to expect.

"I'd rather be prepared for 100 plus than prepped for 80 and find myself low on ammo with an RPG up my arse," he'd said to the other SNCO's.

Cpl Josephs got into position with his new sniper rifle, the L115A3 Accuracy International which fires an 8.59mm round. It is much heavier enabling it to travel greater distances, be more accurate and pierce armour if required to with the right round in it. Josephs had apparently hit a head shot at 1600 metres in training; a head shot at one mile was thought to be a fluke until he repeated the feat minutes later. Despite its official effective range of 1100 metres it was known that several snipers had hit targets at up to 2000 metres, a whopping 2 km. Nothing and no one was safe with that kind of fire power on your side.

Sgt Fisher had laid his section out similarly to King's. He had Cpl Taylor and Cpl Malarkey in one trench which they had dug but was literally six inches deep. The second team was Private Wilson, Private Dunn and Cpl Josephs while the last team included Cpl Harrison, Privates Frost and Stenner along with Fisher moving between the teams as and when required. They were ready and Fisher radioed everyone to let them know. King responded the same, and then Davies, then Riddle and finally Harris gave two clicks on his radio handset to give them the go.

They stared at their watches as the seconds passed by. Bang on time they heard the boom of a tank in the distance firing its 120mm round towards the target and hoped it was accurate enough to do the job in hand. It was, it hit the East wall with pinpoint accuracy blowing chunks of rubble into the complex. Sirens went off notifying the soldiers that they were under attack, as if the huge explosion wasn't enough.

The room shook as the General was about to get up from his chair. Aduor had just called her husband and his colleagues to the dinner table in the next room. The smell was beautiful and the men could hardly wait to get this feast under way.
"Papa," screamed the eldest boy as he hit the floor and crawled under the dining table for cover.

The youngest boy stood there frozen to the

spot, his mother ran to him grabbing him off the ground and into her arms as she shouted to the other to follow her down into the cellar.

At first the General threw himself to the floor as did his advisors, then realising he was under attack he got back to his feet and calmly dusted himself off before speaking.

"I will be downstairs with my family, keep me informed of what is going on and let me know if I'm needed to lead my men."

He turned and walked towards the kitchen to gain access to the cellar and put his family at ease. He sat by his wife's side and took his eldest son in his arms and placed him on his lap.

"It will be alright my sons, everything will be over soon. There isn't an army in the world that can defeat us; we are the kings of our own destiny and we will rule for a thousand years."

Both of his children looked at him with pride, despite being scared of the loud noise which had just occurred. His wife however wasn't so convinced, he had made many enemies over the years but she felt he had crossed the line when he publicly humiliated the British about defeating the Para's. She knew it was more luck than circumstance and she was scared.

After the explosion Davies and Riddle gave it a ten count before moving in on the entrances to the complex. Private Newland set a small charge on the rear gates made from a thick wood, but he knew it was only locked by a large bolt with padlock. Cpl Harvey fired his 66mm LAW into the machine gun post to the left of the main gate while Privates Stone and Cairns opened up with the Gimpy on the right machine gun post obliterating it in seconds. Riddles men got up and made a run for the main entrance, shoot and scoot was the name of the game only they were going forward rather than trying to escape as this technique was usually used.

Harris and his men moved through the drainage system and made it to the cellar area undetected as the noise from the weapons thundered above ground. They got to a point where they could see Gooder's family and staff hiding in the cellar, but they couldn't see Gooder. They didn't have time to feel sorry for the innocent people who might be killed; they had a job to do.

Harris and Brice planted the first charge close to the vent before moving back twenty metres and placing the second. This continued until they had laid all ten charges in the drainage system and headed back to the well in the middle of the courtyard. This would be their access point to the centre of the complex and would kill whoever got in their way.

At the front of the complex Riddle's Pathfinder team were taking men down by the dozen. At the rear, the charge had blown the gates open and Newland and Davies were the first to charge in with all guns blazing, followed closely by Sanders and Stollers. Hands and Stevens were holding the rear to ensure no one outflanked them as the final pair went through the rear gate. Stafford and Bands ran through the gates to be met with an onslaught of gun fire, they quickly hit the ground and tried to find cover but Stafford caught six rounds in his back as he hit the deck. He didn't move, he lay there motionless as Hands looked on in terror.

The sun was rising fast and the light made his eyes water blurring his vision. He saw the gunner firing from a fixed point on the roof of the first building across the yard.

Hands raised his SA80 and fired three rounds into the man standing next to the gunner, he was supplying the ammo which would keep him going but also he couldn't get a clear shot at the gunner without putting himself at risk. Stevens ran across to the other side of the gate, attracting fire from the machine gunner, as this happened they heard the pop of a UGL and the gunner was no more. Smoke and fire bellowed from the rooftop where he had once been. Hand looked across to see Newland smiling back at him and giving him the thumbs up signal.

Hands and Stevens had no choice but to enter the complex to provide support to their team, Stevens grabbed Stafford and dragged his body outside the gate before running back inside firing as he went.

Back at the main entrance Cpl Josephs had just claimed his tenth kill of the day with his sniper rifle, his marksmanship skills are what probably kept Riddle's men alive for so long. Riddle got on the radio and asked for a four man back up team. Fisher responded, "We're on our way, over."

"Roger that," said Riddle sounding relieved.

He knew they were in deep shit but had to stay focused on the job in hand. The success of the mission was vital and he was beginning to have doubts about achieving his goal.

The SAS were using welding gear to cut through the steel mesh which had been put in place on the drainage system into the well, after the last assault caught the enemy off guard. As they were getting through the final section, a member of the enemy forces who had been in the last battle, popped his head over the wall of the well to see sparks flying off into the water below.

He grabbed a grenade from his webbing, but as he did this Pathfinder Private Stone called it in quickly over the radio and the SAS men took cover behind a Kevlar sheet. As soon as the explosion went off Harris kicked out the remaining section of steel mesh into the water below and stuck his head and MP5A3 out into the well. As the enemy soldier looked over a second time to see if he had done any damage Harris was waiting and put two rounds in his head. He flew backwards hitting the ground with force, the dust spat up from around him; his colleagues thought he'd been hit from the gate so didn't bother to check the well.

The four men climbed into the well and scaled its walls to the top, Harris and Brice grabbed a flash bang each and threw them over the wall in the general direction of the enemy soldiers. As the explosion went off all four jumped out of the well and began firing on them.

Riddle called out over the radio, "Man down, man down."

Fisher was already rushing to his aid with Malarkey, Stenner and Dunn. As they got to the gate Stenner fell backwards and as Malarkey looked back he could see a pool of blood mixing with the sand and dirt around his friends head.

Josephs came on the radio, "All men, all men we have a sniper in the complex and I can't see him. He has eyes on the front gate and possibly the courtyard. I have no eyes, over."

"Copy that," Riddle responded, "the man down is Private Gavin Goodwin, over."

"Copy that, over," an unknown voice from HQ responded.

They were listening in to the whole operation and doing nothing about it.

"Man down, man down," came another cry from Davies this time. "Stafford and Newland are down, KIA over."

Kenny couldn't take any more; they had

been laying down covering fire from their position 300 metres away for long enough but couldn't see any of 2 section. He could hear the carnage unfolding inside and felt he had to respond. Riddle came on the radio again sounding anxious.

"We need all men in here. We've got big trouble in little China. They're coming out of the fucking woodwork in here and we're dropping them like no one's business. I need......."

His voice disappeared leaving an eerie silence on the radio.

"Riddle is down, over," the voice of Cpl Harvey sounded gutted, "we're in deep shit in here guys so if anyone out there can hear us we fucking need you in here now, over and out."

The radio burst into life now from Davies, "Kenny I need you in here now mate, we're fucked."

His voice had never sounded so desperate and this wasn't the Sgt Davies he knew, things must have been bad for these guys to be shouting for help as urgent as they were.

Kenny had Bell and Price hang back to cover their escape if they made it back out. He ran for the East wall with four of his men behind him, sending Rust and Harris to the rear to back up Davies and his team. Kenny knew tactics and the enemy figured the East wall was a diversion and after no one coming through it after all this time they thought they were safe to have their backs to the hole in the wall. They were wrong.

Davies and his men were in a real jam as Rust and

Harris arrived at the scene. Harris let rip with a Gimpy tearing the enemies attack apart as Rust let off an 80mm LAW towards the main building behind them.

General Gooder was heading to the roof to command his men; he had decided it was better to die fighting then hiding in a basement with his wife and kids.

Unbeknown to the British soldiers Colonel Igwe and his 100 strong reserve army were on their way. They had a forty minute drive to get to the complex and the battle had being going for fifteen. This was the only saving grace for the men fighting, at this point, not only to take down General Gooder but for their lives.

The radio bursts were short and to the point, they wanted HQ to record any fatalities and keep them updated on the situation.

Sgt Harris came on, "Man down, Trooper Stephen Dunn KIA, over."

After each sitrep (situation report) the simple response came back.

"Copy that, over."

Davies came back on next, "Man down, Private David Brown KIA, over."

The men were dropping like flies in there and Kenny had made his way to the East wall and the access hole created by the tank earlier. He got to the hole and put a man either side while he and Black got into place to go through the access point.

He looked at his friend Black and gave him the kind of look that said it all; they didn't expect to come out of this one alive. They both knew it was a suicide mission but their friends were dying in there and they had to do something.

"On three," Kenny said in a firm tone nodding at his men.

They reciprocated and checked their rifles, "one, two, three, Go! Go! Go!"

Kenny and Black stood up and threw in a grenade each. Black opened up with his LSW while Kenny clambered over the broken wall. He got into cover and started putting down fire with the Minimi while Black followed him into the pit of hell.

The air was full of cordite and smoke and men ran around wildly firing at anything they thought was a threat. Kenny and Black were putting down well placed fire, dropping enemy soldiers. McMann and Harris came running up behind them and got into position so King and Black could move forward and Bands and Rust could gain access. They left Chaplin covering the entrance.

The six men moved like a well oiled machine, the procedures were ingrained in their skulls. They had practised these manoeuvres over and over again in training and the posters they had seen on the walls of Aldershot had been right.

'It's better to sweat on the training ground, than bleed on the battle ground.'

Kenny saw Sgt Harris and his team of troopers trying to fight their way through the courtyard and getting stopped by the sheer volume of men coming out of the cellar, just like last time.

"Fuck this," thought Kenny, "not this time you don't."

He looked back to see where McMann was, "Sandy get your arse up here and prime that pack," shouted King.

"I'm on it," he called back as he ran towards the front while being covered by his oppo, Harris.

The pack was similar to the type suicide bombers used, it was packed with 4 kg of C4 explosives and although not official military protocol, these guys weren't taking any chances this time.

The men continued to put down supporting fire for the SAS team but they couldn't see any of the others. Kenny could still hear the commotion coming from both sides of the complex so he knew it was still kicking off all around him.

After around 60 seconds McMann called out, "We're ready to rock and roll boss!"

"Good, give it here and give me some covering fire."

Kenny didn't wait for anyone to confirm that they were ready, he just went for it. He ran at full speed toward the enemy. A group of around twenty men saw him coming at them and just stopped dead in their tracks not quite knowing what to make of this craziness. As he got within 30 feet of them he opened up with the Minimi taking the majority of them down. Seeing this Cpl Harvey of Pathfinder called his men to give covering fire.

Kenny got within 10 feet of the cellar entrance, snapped the primer setting its 15 second timer off and threw the pack into the cellar. He then turned and looked for cover barely making it behind a small wall when the explosion erupted shaking the building and the ground they stood on.

As Kenny lay there with his ear's ringing from the shock waves he could hear a muffled noise from his radio. It sounded like a panicked Lance Cpl Chaplin; Kenny got to his knees and checked around him. The fighting was still going on all around but there were no more men coming from the cellar.

His hearing came back as quickly as it had left and he heard Chaplin calling over the radio.
"Don't fire, I repeat don't fire. We have men in the East side entrance. Please don't fire, blue on blue!"

Kenny quickly ran towards his men shouting for them to take cover as he heard the boom of the Tank firing its first round toward the complex.

The building rocked as the 120mm round struck taking out another huge section of the building wall. The radio fell silent and small arms fire cracked as a few men carried on fighting despite the explosion and the commotion.

Kenny called out over the radio, "Chaplin are you ok over? Chaplin do you copy over?"

"Kenny," came a voice over the radio, "He didn't stand a fucking chance, it was a direct hit."

"Who's that?" he asked

"It's me Bell," he responded, "is everyone else ok in there?"

"I have no fucking idea, I need to do a quick check and get back to you. Watch our arse and tell that twat to hold his fucking fire, you got me?" Kenny said sharply.

"Got it boss, for anyone listening that was Lance Cpl Chaplin KIA, blue on blue over."

"Copy that, over," said the emotionless voice from HQ.

King and Black got together and started looking for the rest of the team while taking sporadic small arms fire. They thought the worst of it was surely over and the enemy couldn't have much more to give. He knew they didn't.

As he climbed over the rubble in search of his men he caught his first glimpse of 2 section and saw Sgt Davies pinned down behind a burnt out Jeep which still smouldered. As he took a step he stood on a hand and almost fell to the ground, as he looked down he could see the para wings on the shoulder of a man. He bent down and went to take the strain of lifting a man when all that came was a

180

severed arm. He fell back with shock and started to dig frantically.

"Kenny," snapped Black, "we ain't got time for this mate, he's fucking gone."

At that point Kenny unearthed what was left of Private Harris, he had been blown in half and his right arm, shoulder and right side of his rib cage had come away from the rest of his body.

"Kenny," came a faint murmur from a few feet away under more rubble.

Black and King ran to the side of the building to where the voice had come from, and started digging. After a few seconds they found McMann buried under the rubble.

He raised his head and brought his hands up rubbing his eyes.

"Fuck me fella's that C4 pack sure packed a punch didn't it," as he cackled with laughter.

Black started laughing too but Kenny just picked him up and started checking him for injuries.

"I think I'm alright mate," he said surprised, "got bomb blasted the length of the fucking room, bastards."

"Yeah, Harris bought it," said Black.

"Shit, poor kid. Well let's go get some payback," he said smiling.

"Fucking right!" responded Black, King just nodded.

He was clearly struggling with so much loss and they still hadn't found Bands and Rust. As they ran to give cover to Davies they saw two figures creeping across the rear yard area in plain sight of the enemy as if they were blind. The astonishing thing was that they made it all the way across the yard to the building that was pinning 2 section down.

King noticed one of his guys; he had paired up with Cpl Brice from the SAS. Rust looked back and pointed to his throat mike signalling that it was broken. King gave a nod back before putting down covering fire for Davies to move towards their position as much for a breather as anything else.

Davies and Stevens came running into their area collapsing onto the floor before gathering themselves and sitting up to speak.

"Boy am I glad to see you ya big ugly bastard," smiled Davies to King.

"You okay Bri? You look like shit."

"State the fucking obvious why don't ya, yeah I'm tickety fucking boo!"

"You know what I mean ya shit. How many men you got left?"

"Me, Stevens, Hand, Stollers and I think Sanders," he said struggling to think.

Black was firing at the position that had pinned Davies down when a commotion started on the roof top. A body came flying over the top screaming as it fell to the ground. The man's neck snapped as he hit the dirt covered yard and firing could be heard above them.

Rust stood up and stuck his head over the roof edge and shouted to Black while laughing, "You'll never hit me from there you cockeyed twat."

Black turned to the others, "we're in business, let's move."

They grabbed their gear and made a run for the building when they heard Bell's voice boom into life over the radio.

"Fuck me; we've got a convoy of maybe 100 men coming in fast. Four trucks full and they're armed to the fucking teeth by the looks of it. You really need to get the fuck out of there guys," Bell shouted.

Harris came over the radio, "If you lot have finished playing catch up back there we need some fucking support up front. We've got another wave of skinny's coming out of the ground over here, over."

"Roger that, we're on our way," responded Kenny as he gathered a team together. "Stollers, McMann, Black and Stevens, you're coming with me. The rest of you go with Bri and take those fucking buildings. We need the high ground if we're gonna take these fuckers."

King moved quickly to his previous position when he heard Bell for a second time calling to the tank for it to hold its fire from the complex and aim at the convoy. Thankfully on this occasion someone seemed to be listening. Kenny stopped in his tracks and watched the tank turret turning away and he breathed a sigh of relief.

Cpl Josephs had to move position several times to avoid the bombardment of mortar fire that was being thrown at him. They desperately wanted to remove the threat of this very talented soldier. He had to hold his fire for twenty five minutes so the enemy would think he was dead before taking up position again. He watched as more enemy poured from the cellar and he took one steady shot after another killing no less than thirty men before having to let his rifle cool down. He had fired a total of 300 rounds during the fire fight and the barrel was almost glowing. Despite its quality no rifle could fire continuously without starting to falter.

Sgt Harris and Trooper Williams of the SAS had finally managed to move forward and dropped eight grenades into the cellar before calling to King and his men.

"We're going down there. We've got to stop these fuckers or we're in the shit. Watch out for that fucking tank, he's determined to finish us off today," he shouted smiling.

King nodded and kept charging towards them; Black looked on with disbelief at the men of the Special Forces. He thought they were crazy to go down into the cellar, it was suicide for sure.

King and Black took up position over the cellar entrance to make sure no-one came back out. McMann and Stollers went for the main building trying to gain entry but came under heavy fire from within.

The windows seemed to erupt into a frenzy of gun fire; Cpl Stevens saw this and sent a 66mm in through one of the large windows directly in front of the men. The explosion took out dozens of enemy soldiers and gave the men time to reach the front of the building and lob a couple of flash bangs in through the window before standing up and letting rip on fully automatic with their rifles.

McMann went through two magazines before entering the building while Stollers gave them everything he had with a Minimi, covering each other as they gained entry to the main living quarters of General Gooder and his family.

Meanwhile the cellar had gone ballistic! The sound was deafening as the SAS troopers fought like men possessed to gain the upper hand. Harris could see a large hole in the wall at the far side of the cellar; this was obviously the entry point for the endless stream of enemy fighters.

Cpl Brice wanted to get in on the action too, he couldn't bear the thought of his comrades falling without him by their sides. He was holding the well and had the charges set to go off at a moment's notice.

"Oi you," Brice called to Stevens, "come here and take care of this for me while I go get myself shot, will ya."

Stevens scurried over to the well and got a quick update on what to do and when to do it from Cpl Brice. He then ran to the cellar entrance to follow the others, "Move over gents, madman coming through. What a beautiful fucking war eh."

He smiled and followed Harris and Williams into the jaws of the enemy stronghold. He quickly came into contact with the others and he too noticed the entry point for the enemy and got out his LAW 66mm and opened it out. It was as if the whole of the enemy force heard the tube slide into the open position as they stopped firing for a moment and held their breaths. He shouldered the weapon and fired it at the hole in the wall killing dozens of enemy and slowing their attack down considerably. But as he threw the tube to the ground and smiled at his friends to celebrate, one of General Gooder's elite bodyguards jumped through the smouldering wall armed with an AK47 and fired a full magazine into Brice. His body danced as the rounds ripped through his flesh tearing him limb from limb.

Harris quickly jumped up and put three rounds into the bodyguards head ending the onslaught of fire into his friend and colleague.

Williams got up and in typical SAS fashion.

"Fuck it!"

He ran towards the hole in the wall. He unleashed a vicious attack firing from the hip as he ran taking no caution as he ran into the enemies face. The enemy were dwindling in numbers as they awaited the arrival of Colonel Igwe and his men.

The tank had managed to take out two of the trucks and most of its personnel, reducing their numbers to around 60 but these men were heading towards the complex on foot and the tank couldn't get its accuracy on target to take out foot soldiers.

Chapter 12

Cpl Josephs was doing his best to slow the reinforcements down but there were just too many of them. He managed to take out 12 men but his rifle was losing accuracy causing him to miss and he couldn't afford for that to happen, so when he saw a large number of enemy reach the rear entrance of the complex he decided to leave his sniper rifle booby trapped with a grenade under it and pick up his assault rifle, the M16 A2 with UGL. He loaded up his gear, grabbed a snickers bar and a drink of water before setting off to the front building.

King and his men could hear firing all around the main building and they hoped their friends would make it through. Meanwhile Sgt Harris and Trooper Williams continued to fight below ground; it was amazing that they hadn't been killed as they encountered fight after fight.

King looked up at the roof of the main building which McMann and Stollers were storming and saw Gooder and his men on the roof. They began firing on the Paratroopers below and they were forced to dive for cover. Gooder was a good shot so it was no surprise that it didn't take him long to find his first target.

Stevens didn't see it coming; he took two rounds through his neck. Blood squirted from his jugular in time with his beating heart and he knew his time was coming to an end. There was no way a medic would get to him in time and so he looked at Kenny and tried calling out to him.

"Got to blow it."

King however was trying to take out the enemy on the roof and didn't hear or see what was happening to Stevens. Black just happened to turn and see Stevens going for the detonator and shouted to him.

"STOP!"

As Stevens crawled to the detonator and placed it in his hand the final shot rang out across the yard and he lay still in the dirt with blood slowly pumping from his throat as a pool began to gather from behind him. The final round had come from Gooder, it entered his body just below the ribcage tearing through his lung and out through his back rupturing his spine killing him instantly.

Black called to King, "Kenny we need to get those guys out of there and blow this fucking thing to shit!"

"We don't even know if they're still alive but let me get in that building. I'm gonna mess that bastard up once and for all," shouted Kenny, "Give me three minutes then blow the thing to shit and get the fuck out of here and I mean get out of here. That's a fucking order, get it."

"Get fucked I'm coming in with ya," screamed Black.

They both got to their feet and ran for the

building making it unscathed. Kenny threw caution to the wind and jumped straight in through the front window without checking it first, Black knew this was the sign of a man ready to die and followed without question.

Josephs took up position next to the well and shot three of Gooder's men on the roof within seconds of getting there.

Meanwhile the tank commander decided it was time to finish things up and leave, he fired three rounds in quick succession to the rear of the complex where he'd seen the bulk of enemy soldiers enter the grounds. As they made contact the ground shook and King and Black fell flat on their faces. As Kenny looked ahead he came face to face with the cold dead eyes of Lance Cpl Stollers. He lay in a pool of black blood riddled with bullets holes in his torso; he must have been hit at least thirty times. There was no sign of McMann as of yet. They continued on through the building trying to gain access to the roof. As they got closer they could hear small arms fire from a Minimi and hoped it was McMann doing what he did best, kicking ass.

They reached the corner of a long corridor and Black called out.

"Airborne!"

"Get your arse round here," shouted McMann, he was glad to be joined by someone else.

He was struggling to hold them off; he had made it to the exit route to the roof but was

190

running low on ammo and couldn't gain access to the roof to finish the job in hand. Black crouched low and ran across to McMann's side and immediately opened up on the guards killing two.

"Fall back and grab a breather, Kenny is around the corner watching the rear."

"King," shouted McMann, "never mind hiding round the fucking corner, get your arse round here and kill some of these bastards."

Kenny turned the corner and smiled, as from out of nowhere a huge black enemy soldier came charging from out of one of the side rooms at Kenny with a rifle and fixed bayonet. He screamed his war cry as he threw his weight at King, the blade of the bayonet sliced through the front part of Kenny's shoulder tearing the muscle from the bone.

He screamed with pain and lashed out with his left fist making contact with the giant mans jaw. The crunch of his teeth could be heard over the noise as he fell sideways under the force of the blow. Kenny quickly snatched the bayonet and pulled it out of his shoulder dropping it to the floor. The soldier, still dazed from the strike fumbled around the floor for the weapon but Kenny stamped on his hands repeatedly.

The enemy soldier, a man called Igwe grabbed Kenny's ankle throwing him to the ground and they grappled with each other while Black and McMann could do nothing. They were coming under heavy fire from the troops on the roof.

Igwe got Kenny's back and wrapped his huge forearm around his neck trying to strangle him but Kenny bit him hard breaking the skin. In response to this the giant man didn't let go, instead he took a bite out of Kenny's Trapezius muscle from behind taking a chunk of flesh in his teeth. Blood flooded the back of his jacket to match the wound to the front. It was the same side he had been stabbed moments earlier.

As the men fought and rolled around the floor there was a huge explosion, then came the shock wave and the entire building shook before half of the main building collapsed under the pressure. Cpl Josephs had no option but to set off the detonators the SAS soldiers had placed before the raid began.

The enemy replacements were overrunning the courtyard and he couldn't hold them back any longer. He fired his last round and set off the detonators before attempting to make a run for the front gates. The tunnel ran directly under the area he was running across collapsing under him. As he lay amongst the rubble Colonel Igwe appeared and looked down on him, raised his handgun and shot him three times in the chest. As he turned to instruct his men to get up and search the area for survivors Sgt Harris of the SAS stood before him with an AK 47 in his hands.

Harris quickly raised the rifle and fired three

rounds into the head of the Colonel. He turned and looked at the building ruins in front of him and wondered if anyone had survived. Trooper Williams had died fighting to gain ground in the cellar, seeing this Harris realised he was about to die when he heard an English voice calling for backup. He turned and ran to his aid fighting his way back up to the surface just before the explosion went off. He was too late to save the man calling for help, Cpl Steve Taylor was shot in the head just as Harris reached him. He did however manage to return the favour before the explosion knocked everyone off their feet by putting two rounds in the enemy soldier's chest.

After witnessing the destruction of the complex from a distance, Bell and Price ran to the East wall and entered at the same point as the rest of the team had earlier. They quickly made their way to the main building and started to look for the men who were inside. To their amazement they heard a shout from above them. In the half of the building that was still standing they looked up to see McMann hanging from a window ledge on the inside of the building with a twenty foot drop below him. He couldn't quite reach the floor which was situated four feet to his left.

Bell, Price and Bands climbed the ruin to help McMann when they heard Kenny shout.
"He's getting away."

Harris turned to see King buried with his head and

left arm peering out of the rubble. He struggled to drag himself out enough to take aim; he could see Gooder and two of his bodyguards making a run for a jeep some thirty yards away behind the building. He picked up a Galil Assault Rifle, checked it was loaded and rested it on a large piece of the building rubble and fired one shot. It struck guard number one in the back of the head sending him spinning head over heels, he then took another breath and fired again, this time at guard number two. The single shot hit him square between the shoulder blades, the man twitched for a few seconds before remaining still.

General Gooder turned to see the assassin who had taken out his men and shouted.
"Who do you think you are? Who the fuck are you?"

Kenny raised the rifle to his left shoulder and put three rounds into General Gooder's head. His body spun around and hit the ground heavily as brain tissue spilled into the dirt and sand around him.

He crawled from under the debris raising the rifle in the air with his left arm and shouted.
"I AM SOLDIER!!!" He calmed his breathing before mumbling to himself, "That's who the fuck I think I am."

Kenny scrambled amongst the rubble and picked up his red beret placing it on his head with pride. He looked across to the other survivors; Sgt Harris was the only SAS survivor, of the

Pathfinders Cpl Harvey, Private Stone and Private Cairns made it out alive but not without injury. Cairns had lost his foot and there were doubts if he would keep his leg, time would tell.

Kenny felt the earth to his left move and saw the huge enemy soldier Igwe raise his head and look at him; he grabbed a chunk of rock and smashed it into his face several times before breaking down.

The Scots Guards arrived by Chinook, fifty men came running to the Para's rescue. They were too late; many lives had been sacrificed to rid the dictator General Gooder from power.
From 1 section Sgt Fisher, Cpl Malarkey, Private's Frost, Harrison, Wilson and Dunn survived. 2 section Sgt Davies although seriously injured survived along with Cpl Bands, Private's Hand and Sanders and finally 3 section Sgt Kenny King, Cpl Rust and Private's Black, McMann, Bell and Price made it out alive.

Major Silvers, Captain Briar and 2nd Lt Mellor had heard the battle unfold over the radio and felt helpless as they struggled to arrange a rescue mission.

The men of the Scots Guards ran around the remains of the complex searching for the missing Paratroopers, rounding up enemy survivors and shooting those who put up a fight.

They looked on in disbelief at the death and destruction that surrounded them. A Royal Marine

Officer, Captain Milford walked over to Sgt Harris enquiring if Cpl Josephs was around. Harris pointed to the collapsed tunnel and the body of the dead marine who had fought so valiantly.

Black was found sitting on a pile of rubble near the well staring into space with lines down his face from the tears he'd shed. He was holding a heavily bandaged left hand when the Guards medic got to him. He had lost two fingers in the building collapse and had broken several ribs.

A little while later King staggered over and sat down next to his friend on a mound of rubble just outside the front gates of what was a fortress built to protect a dictator. They didn't speak, they didn't need to. They had known each other a long time; Kenny was also waiting to be medicated after the bayonet injury, the medic was worried he might lose his arm or be unable to use it again. It was his right shoulder and they wanted to get him treatment ASAP.

Kenny, although not a religious man, sat thinking for a while and wondered if God would forgive him for all the killing he had done on this day, he couldn't bring himself to cry although he wanted to. He felt pain inside yet no remorse for those who had died; it is a strange feeling to feel such indifference.

He sat with the warm sun beating down on his face and wondered, what was next.....

<u>Glossary</u>

APC	Armoured Personnel Carrier
Bergen	Large Military Rucksack
Browning	9mm Pistol
C 130	Hercules aircraft
Capt	Captain
Civi	Civilian
CO	Commanding Officer
Coy	Company
CP	Command Post
Cpl	Corporal
Crap hat	Any soldier not from Para Reg
CSM	Company Sergeant Major
CTR	Close Target Recce
DZ	Drop Zone
ERV	Emergency Rendezvous
ETA	Expected Time of Arrival
Flash Bang	White Phosphorus Grenade
FOB	Forward Operating Base
Gimpy	General Purpose Machine Gun (GPMG)
Green Slime	Intelligence Corps
HQ	Head Quarters
Intel	Intelligence
IRA	Irish Republican Army
KIA	Killed in action
LAW	Light Anti-tank Weapon
L115A3	Accuracy International 8.59mm

	Sniper Rifle
L96A1	Accuracy International 7.62mm Sniper Rifle
LSW	Light Support Weapon
Lt	Lieutenant
LUP	Lying up position
MC	Military Cross
Milling	'Controlled aggression' in a milling contest - similar to boxing, except neither winning, losing, nor skill are pre-requisites of passing. Candidates are instead scored on their determination, while blocking and dodging result in points deducted. Candidates now wear head protection and gum shields as well as boxing gloves.
Minimi LMG	5.56mm Light Machine Gun
MP	Military Police
M16	US assault rifle used by SF & PF
M203	Underslung grenade launcher attached under M16
M60	American GPMG
NAAFI	Navy Army Air Force Institute
NCO	Non-Commissioned Officer
NI	Northern Ireland
NLAW	Next Generation Light Anti-tank weapon
NVG	Night vision goggles
Op	Operation

OP	Observation Post
Para	Paratrooper
PF	Pathfinder
PIRA	Provisional Irish Republican Army
PJI	Parachute Jump Instructor
PMG	Soviet 7.62 mm Pecheneg machine guns
Pte	Private
QGM	Queens Gallantry Medal
RAF	Royal Air Force
Recce	Reconnaissance
Reg	Regiment
RMC	Royal Marines Commando
R & R	Rest & Recuperation
RSM	Regimental Sergeant Major
RTU'd	Returned to unit
RV	Rendezvous
SA80	Standard-issue British Army Rifle
SAS	Special Air Service
SBS	Special Boat Service
SF	Special Forces
SFC	Sergeant First Class (American equivalent)
Sgt	Sergeant
Sitrep	Situation Report
SNCO	Senior Non-Commissioned Officer
SOP	Standard Operating Procedure
SUSAT	Sight Unit Small Arms Trilux
TAB	Tactical Advance to Battle – the army's name for moving at speed carrying a heavy Bergen

UGL	Underslung Grenade Launcher
Utrinque Paratus	The Parachute Regiment's motto meaning 'Ready for Anything'
WO	Warrant Officer – the most senior NCO rank. Either a Company or Regimental Sergeant Major
2IC	Second in Command

Printed in Great Britain
by Amazon.co.uk, Ltd.,
Marston Gate.